George B. Kilbon

Carpentry for Boys

Elementary Woodwork - a series of lessons designed to give fundamental

instruction in use of all the principal tools needed in carpentry and joinery

George B. Kilbon

Carpentry for Boys
Elementary Woodwork - a series of lessons designed to give fundamental instruction in use of all the principal tools needed in carpentry and joinery

ISBN/EAN: 9783337377588

Printed in Europe, USA, Canada, Australia, Japan

Cover: Foto ©Andreas Hilbeck / pixelio.de

More available books at **www.hansebooks.com**

CARPENTRY FOR BOYS

ELEMENTARY WOODWORK

A SERIES OF LESSONS

DESIGNED TO GIVE FUNDAMENTAL INSTRUCTION IN USE OF ALL THE PRINCIPAL TOOLS NEEDED IN CARPENTRY AND JOINERY

BY

GEORGE B. KILBON

PRINCIPAL OF MANUAL TRAINING, SPRINGFIELD, MASS., AND AUTHOR OF "KNIFE WORK IN THE SCHOOLROOM"

Illustrated

BOSTON

LEE AND SHEPARD PUBLISHERS

10 MILK STREET

1893

CONTENTS.

INTRODUCTION.

The title given to this book was chosen because of the purpose to present fundamental exercises in a simple form for the use of beginners. Effort has been made to detail operations minutely, hoping to be of service to novices, though well aware that no book can be a substitute for an efficient instructor. The arrangement is from the easy to the difficult by successive steps, and is designed to give boys of twelve years and upward primary command of the use of a set comprising the principal wood-working tools. The smaller planes and saws are chiefly used. Other tools are of standard size. Small pieces of wood are used, since elementary instruction can be better given thereby. The different kinds of nail-driving, and the use of gauge and try-square, are first taught on boards prepared by machinery. The ability to use each tool should be mastered before undertaking the study of another.

The lessons described have been given to the ninth, or senior, grammar grade of the public schools at Springfield, Mass., since the organization of the manual training-school at that place in 1886, classes of twelve to nineteen receiving one lesson per week of one and one-half hours' duration, and commencing with September. 1892, the first half of them are now given to the eighth grade, classes receiving one lesson each fortnight. A selection under the title "Ten Lessons in

Manual Training" was published in *The New York School Journal* between Sept. 26, 1891, and Aug. 26, 1892.

The sixth and seventh grades at Springfield receive manual instruction through the medium of knife-work outlined in a book published by The Milton Bradley Co., entitled "Knife Work in the School Room;" the eighth and ninth grades, through the medium of the within described elementary course; and high school pupils who so elect receive daily lessons for three years in joinery, wood-turning, carving, pattern-making, moulding, forging, iron-filing, turning and planing, and machine construction.

The question is under advisement of writing out a description of high-school work following the method pursued in "Knife Work" and in this book. Whether it will be done will depend somewhat on the acceptance of these two volumes.

Mechanical drawing is given to pupils in the eighth and ninth grades in the ordinary schoolroom, using the 9 in. × 12 in. industrial drawing kit made by the Milton Bradley Co.; and among other things drawn are the manual problems. High-school pupils have an extended course of daily work in drawing, their manual problems being included.

EQUIPMENT.

Fig. 1 is a front elevation; Fig. 2, a plan; Figs. 3 and 4, left and right elevations, of an individual work bench, 4½ ft. long × 2 ft. wide × 34 in. high. The two end views show

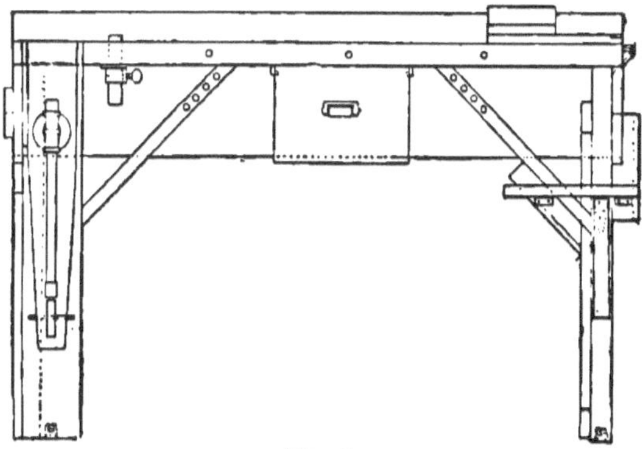

Fig. 1.

tools hanging in position. Other tools are kept, some on the bench top, some in the rack on the back side of the bench, and others in the drawer.

To accommodate boys of small stature, movable platforms 4½ ft. long × 2 ft. wide are used, varying in height from 2 in. to 5 in. When not needed, these platforms are buttoned to the back side of the bench. When the arm of a pupil hangs naturally by the side, and the wrist is bent so as to cause the hand to stand at right angles to the body, the hand so held

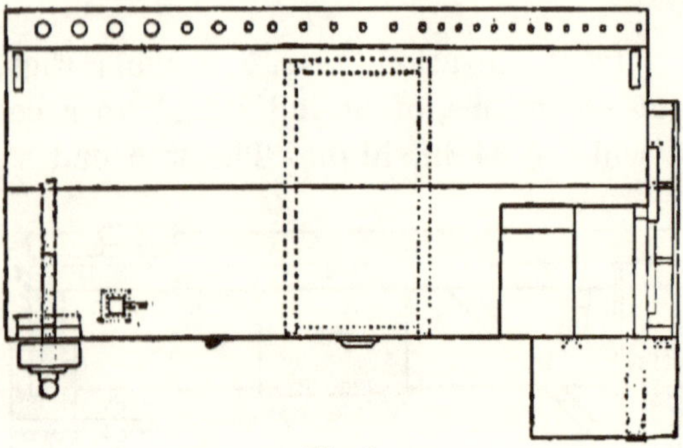

Fig. 2.

should pass just underneath the 2 in. plank forming the top of the bench. This rule will decide the height of platform needed for any pupil.

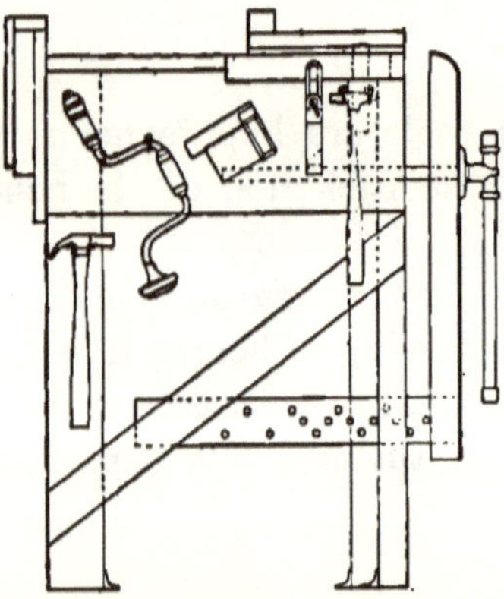

Fig. 3.

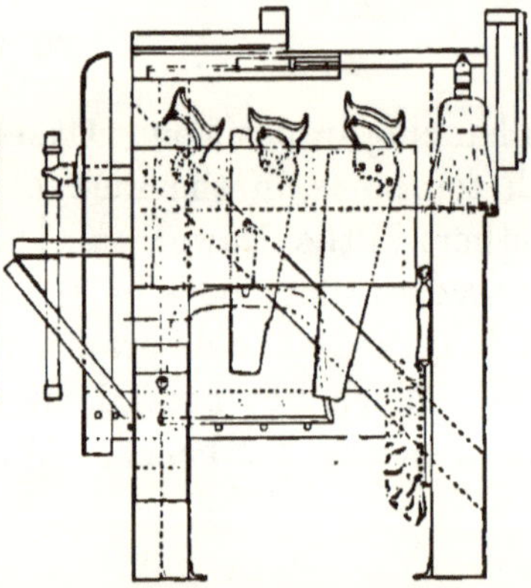

Fig. 4.

A school may be furnished with twelve to twenty-five such benches, according to room or demand. If twenty-five are furnished, and if room allows, a convenient arrangement of them is shown in Fig. 5, each bench being supplied with a stool which the pupil occupies when necessary, and which are gathered around the teacher's desk during class instruction as in Fig. 5.

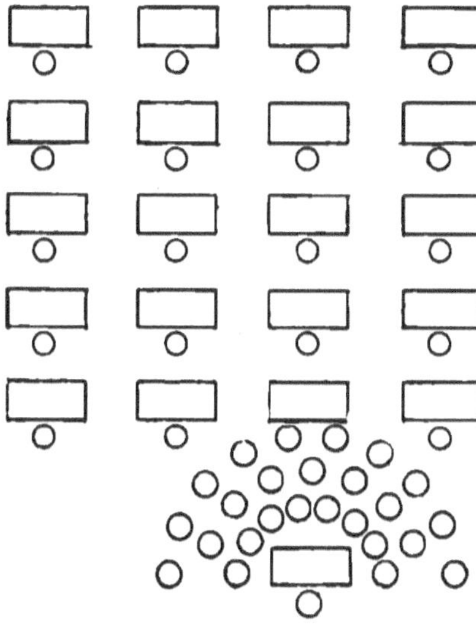

Fig. 5.

LIST OF TOOLS WITH WHICH EACH BENCH IS SUPPLIED, WITH THEIR LOCATION ABOUT THE BENCH.

On the Bench Top.

8 in. Bailey Iron smooth-plane. 6 in. Bailey Iron block-plane. Straight edge 16 in. × 2 in. × 3–16 in. Box 6 in. × 3 in. × 1 in. with four spaces for holding nails. Oil-stone. Oil-can. Anvil 3 in. diam. × 1 in. high. 8 in. wooden smooth-plane. Shove-plane board.

In the Rack.

Brad-awl. 6 in. dividers adjustable for pencil. 5½ in. pliers. Gauge. 3 in. screw-driver. Four firmer chisels 1 in., ½ in., ¼ in., and ⅛ in. Knife with two blades.

On the Right End.

18 in. cutting-off saw. 18 in. slitting-saw. 10 in. back-saw. Saw-block, for use on bench top. Dust brush for use on bench top. Whisk broom for clothing. Rule 12 in. long in one unbroken piece. Saw shelf, hinged to let down when not in use.

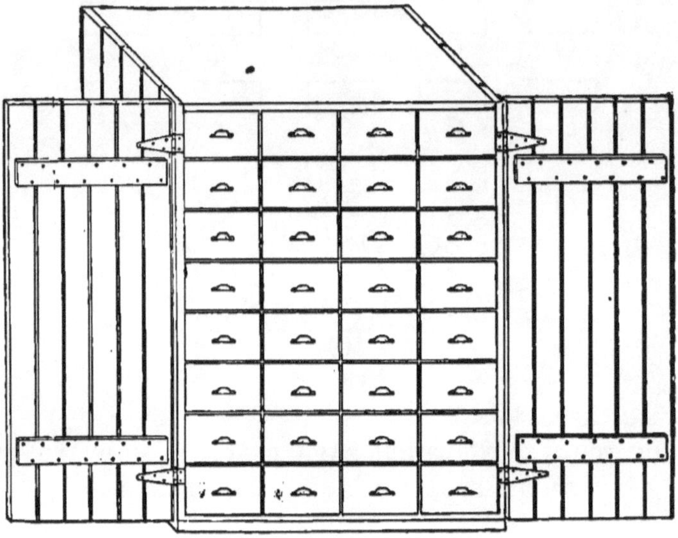

Fig. 6.

On the Left End.

Claw-hammer for driving and drawing nails. Small peen hammer for brads. Try-square, 4 in. blade. Bevel, 6 in. blade. Bit-brace.

In the Drawer.

In a till with partitions to separate them, one $\frac{1}{2}$ in. gouge, inside ground, one $\frac{3}{4}$ in. gouge, outside ground. Three auger bits, $\frac{3}{4}$ in.. $\frac{3}{8}$ in., and $\frac{1}{4}$ in. Two drill-bits, 7–32 in., and 5–32 in. Countersink. Lead-pencil. Eraser. Nail set. Brad set.

Under the till a mallet, and space where all of the tools can be packed when necessary.

Under the Bench.

10 in. hand-clamp. Dust pan and broom for floor-sweeping. Half-bushel basket to hold shavings.

An addition to the foregoing equipment of a half-dozen framing-squares and 22 in. Bailey Iron jointers, and two 26 in. hand-saws will be very serviceable.

Make as many drawers 21 in. × 10 in. × 7½ in. inside measurement as there are to be pupils. Fig. 6 is a perspective view of a cupboard containing 32 such drawers.

LESSON I.

USE OF HAMMER.—NAIL-DRIVING.

The hammer consists of two parts, the head and the handle.

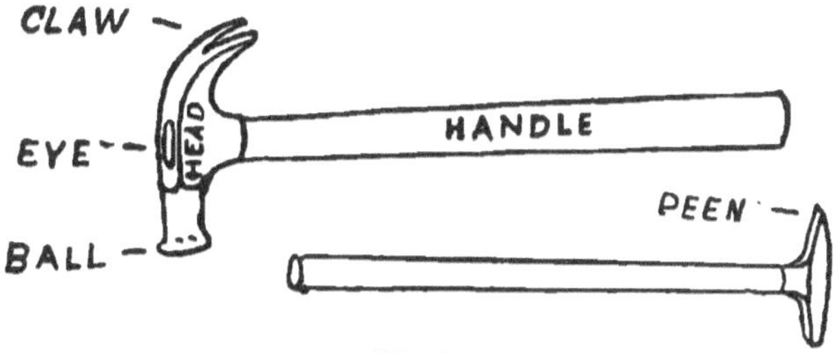

Fig. 7.

The head has three divisions. First, the ball, which is the end that strikes a blow. Second, the eye, or the hole which receives the handle; and third, the claw of the nail-hammer, or peen of the brad-hammer.

Problem I. Driving Steel-Wire Nails.—Take for each pupil a block of pine or other soft wood, 8 in. $\times$ $1\frac{7}{8}$ in. $\times$ $1\frac{7}{8}$ in. On one side draw three pencil lines, as in Fig. 8, and place

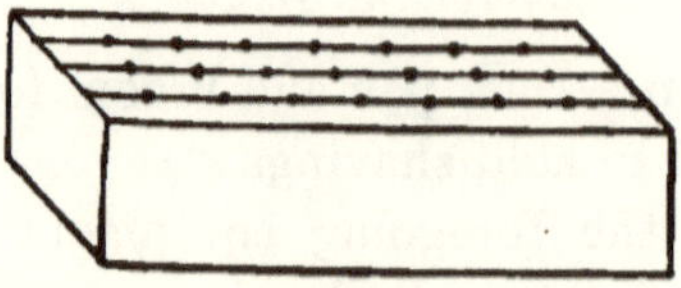

Fig. 8.

points 1 in. apart on each line. Supply each pupil with $1\frac{1}{2}$ dozen 6d. steel-wire nails.

Hold the hand as in Fig. 9, with the thumb on the upper

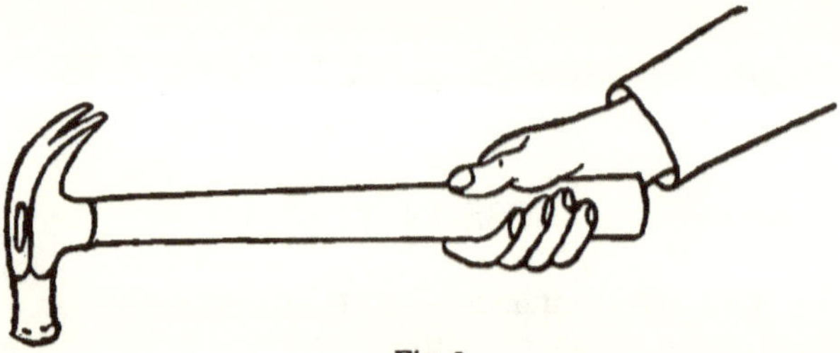

Fig. 9.

side of the handle, or as in Fig. 10, with the hand turned so as to bring the thumb partially to one side. Fig. 9 is the

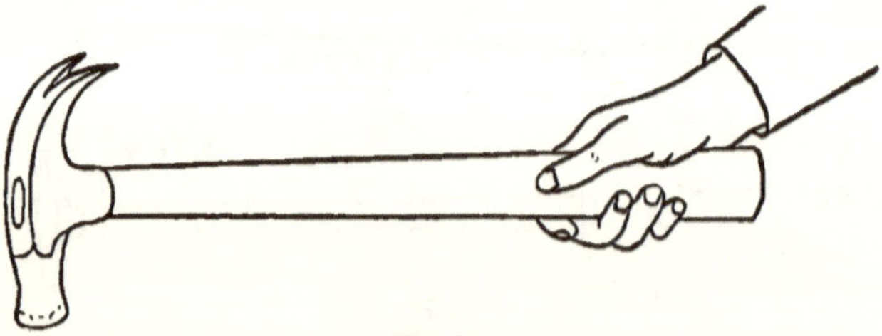

Fig. 10.

scientific position, as the thumb is the stronger digit, while Fig. 10 is more convenient in practice. The forefinger should not rest on the top of the handle, as many amateurs are tempted to do. The end of the handle should project about an inch beyond the hand.

At each of the extreme points on one of the lines in Fig. 8 hold a nail vertical and strike it once. If the blow has caused it to incline, push it back a little past a vertical position, and, holding it there, strike it again. If it continues to incline, it must be loosened in order to press it to a vertical position. Drive each nail until only $\frac{5}{8}$ in. of it projects above the block, as in Fig. 11. At each of the intervening points on the same line drive nails, sighting with the eye to see that the heads are all in line, as in Fig. 12.

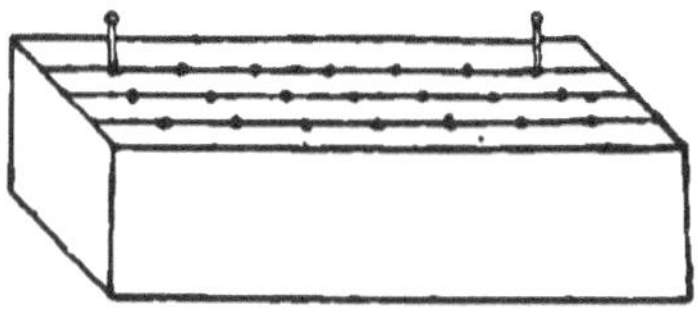

Fig. 11.

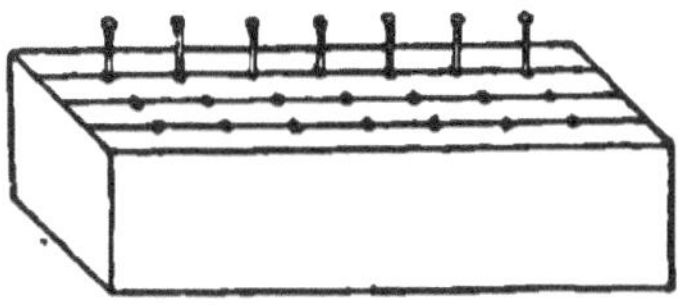

Fig. 12.

Rapid workmen may drive a second row. If it is deemed desirable to mark the work, mark 10 off from 100, for every nail which inclines $\frac{1}{8}$ in. from perpendicular, or whose head is $\frac{1}{16}$ in. above or below the line of $\frac{5}{8}$ in. in height.

Problem II. Drawing Steel-Wire Nails.—Place the work in the vise, with its top level with the bench top, as in Fig. 13.

Supply each pupil with a fulcrum block 8 in. × $1\frac{1}{2}$ in. × $\frac{7}{8}$ in. Hold the hammer as in Fig. 13, supporting its *eye* on the *thickness* of the fulcrum block, and draw the nail about $\frac{5}{8}$ of an inch, moving the hand through about $\frac{1}{8}$ of a circle; that is, to a vertical position, as in Fig. 14.

Support the *eye* on the *width* of the block, as in Fig. 15, and draw the nail entirely from the wood. The eye of a hammer should always be supported thus when drawing nails. The support should be a little higher than the nail head when any

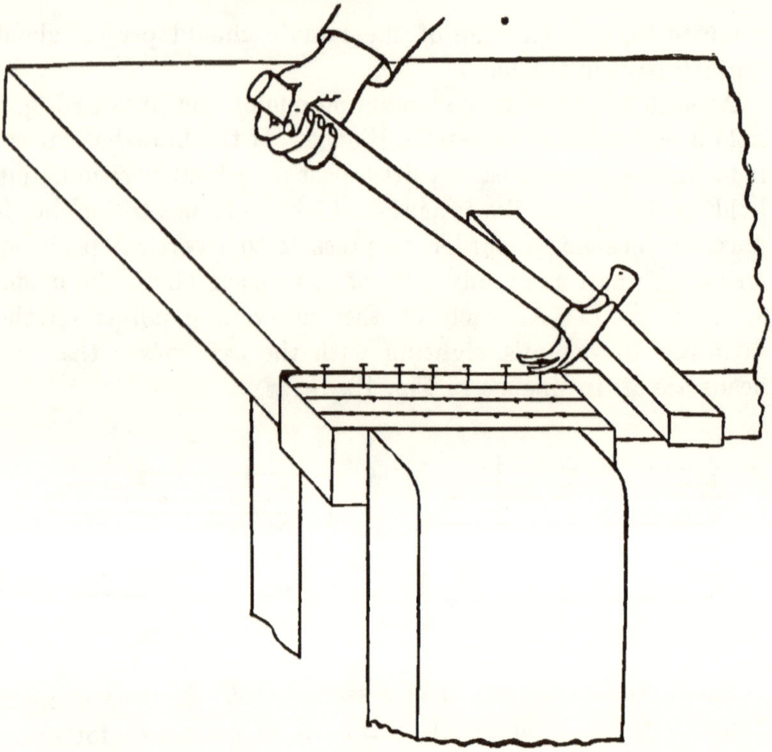

Fig. 13.

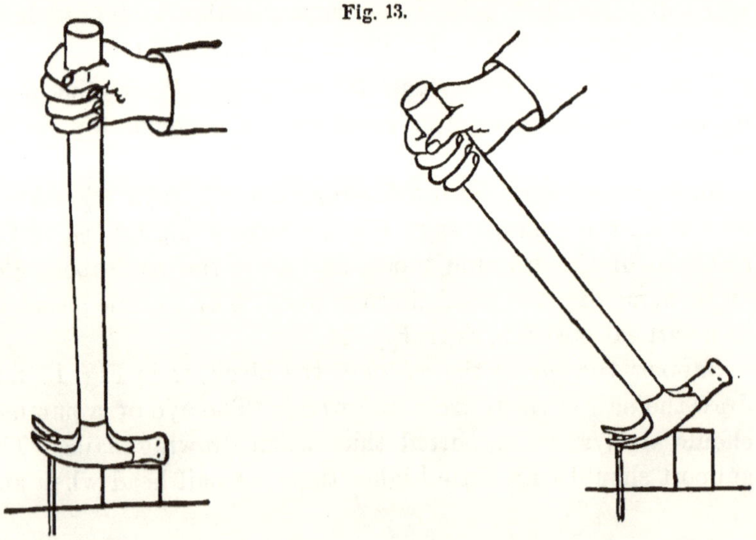

partial drawing commences, and each partial drawing should be about ½ in. to ⅝ in. in amount, in order not to bend the nail, or strain the hammer handle. I have seen workmen break hammer handles and nails resist drawing when neither would have occurred had the above simple direction been followed. Mark 10 off from 100 for every bent nail.

Problem III. Driving Cut Nails.—Upon another side of the block used in the two last problems, draw lines as before and drive 6d. cut nails. These are wedge-shaped viewed from one side, while of uniform thickness viewed from the adjacent side. Insert them as in Fig. 16, in order that they may not split the wood, which will be the case if they are turned ¼ the way around.

Follow the order given in Problem I. and drive one row. Follow the order given in Problem II. and draw them without bending. If any nails do become inadvertently or carelessly bent, straighten them on the anvil. Mark as in previous problems.

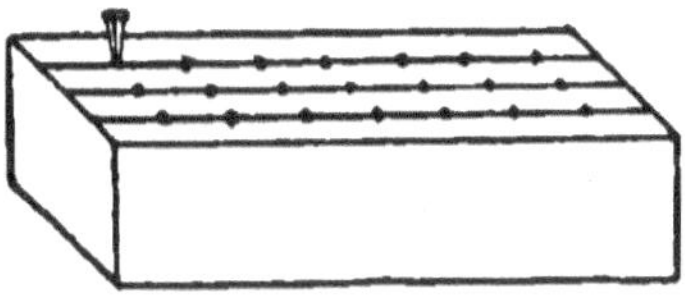

Fig. 16.

Fig. 17.

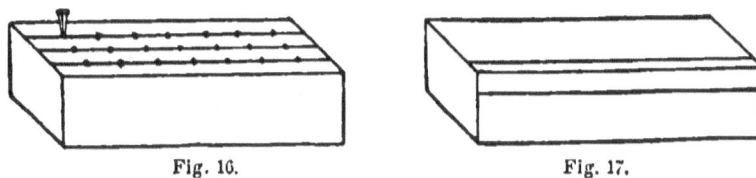

Problem IV. Curve-Nailing.—Take the block used in the previous problems, draw a line on one side ¼ in. from the edge, and place points at every inch upon it. On an adjacent side draw a line ½ in. from the edge, as in Fig. 17

Provide 1 in. No. 18 steel-wire nails. Using the pliers, bend

Fig. 18.

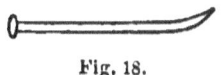

a nail about ⅛ in. from the point, as in Fig. 18. Insert the nail in one of the prepared points on the first side of the block, with its body standing perpendicular, as in Fig. 19, where an end view of the block is shown.

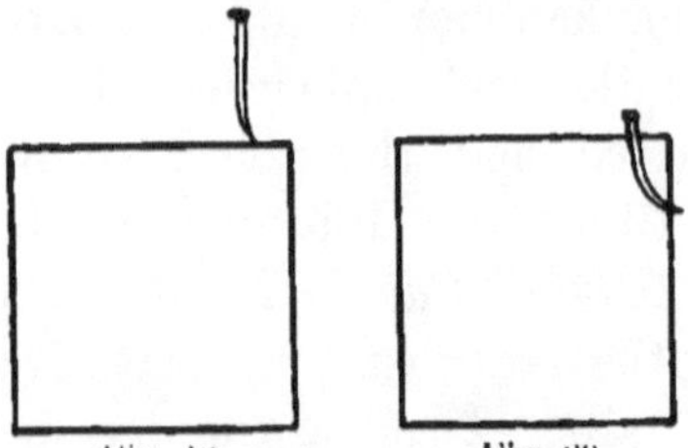

Fig. 19. Fig. 20.

Drive the nail carefully, causing the point to appear on the $\frac{1}{2}$ in. line on the adjacent side of the block, as in Fig. 20. In a similar manner drive nails at the other prepared points, which are on the first side of the block. Mark 10 off from 100 for every nail whose point appears $\frac{1}{8}$ in. from the line on the adjacent side.

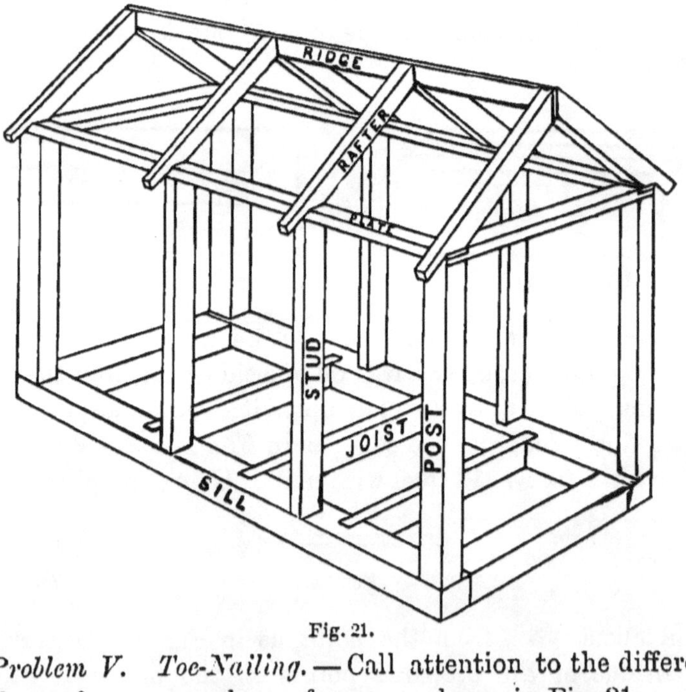

Fig. 21.

Problem V. Toe-Nailing.—Call attention to the different timbers of a common house-frame, as shown in Fig. 21.

These timbers are largely fastened together by a process called toe-nailing.

Take a piece of soft wood 2 in. × 2 in. × $\frac{7}{8}$ in. to represent a sill, and a piece 2 in. × $\frac{7}{8}$ in. × $\frac{7}{8}$ in. to represent a post or stud. Lay the post on the bench, and with the peen hammer

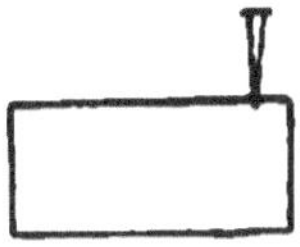

Fig. 22.

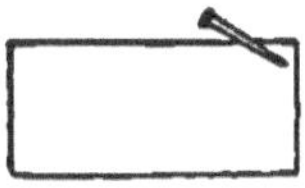

Fig. 23.

start a $\frac{5}{8}$ in. finishing-nail, or patent brad, $\frac{1}{4}$ in. from one end, as in Fig. 22, remembering the relation its wedge shape needs to bear to the grain of the wood.

Press it to an angle of 30° with the side of the post, and drive it well in, but not so as to have the points show on the end. The front view will appear as in Fig. 23. Turn the post so as to bring the bottom side uppermost and supporting it on two blocks, 4 in. × $\frac{11}{16}$ in. × $\frac{5}{16}$ in., which are to be used in the next problem; start another nail in similar manner, as in Fig. 24.

Fig. 24.

Hold the post erect on the sill, and joining the outer faces of the two perfectly, drive both brads as far as possible without marring the wood with the hammer. Hold the left hand firmly on the top of the post while doing this, and do not let perfect joining of faces be disturbed. With the brad set and hammer drive the brads till the heads are flush with the side of the post; that is, till the heads have fully entered the wood. The work will appear as in Fig. 25. One nail-head only is shown in this figure, the other being on the invisible side.

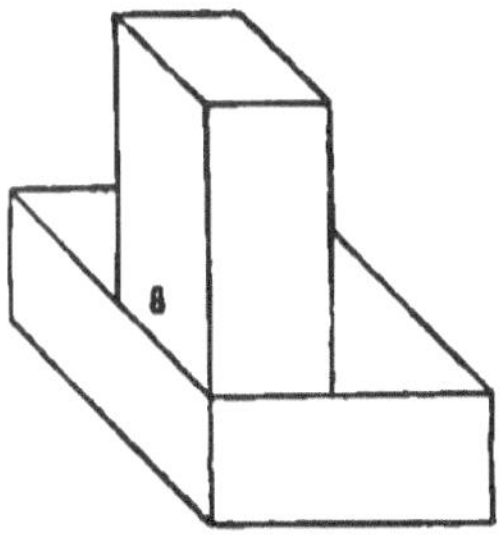

Fig. 25.

In a similar manner start, drive, and set a brad in each of the other sides of the post, when it will be secured to the sill by four brads.

Rapid workmen may perform two or even three problems while the slowest workmen are performing one. Mark 10 off from 100 on each problem for every imperfect joining of faces and for every side of the post that is marred by the hammer.

Problem V. Blind Nailing.—Supply each pupil with two pieces of soft wood 4 in. × $\frac{11}{16}$ in. × $\frac{5}{16}$ in. to represent joists, one piece 4 in. × 2 in. × $\frac{5}{16}$ in. to hold them together conveniently, and five matched boards, 4 in. × $\frac{3}{4}$ × $\frac{1}{4}$ in.

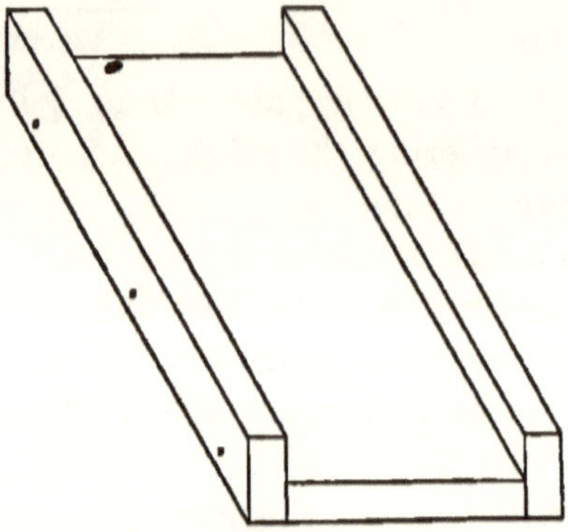

Fig. 26.

Use $\frac{5}{8}$ patent brads, and nail the joists to the board, as in Fig. 26. Place one matched board on the joists with its

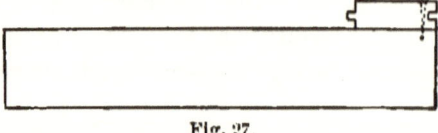

Fig. 27.

grooved edge agreeing with the end of the joists, and drive two brads near the grooved edge of the board, securing it thus

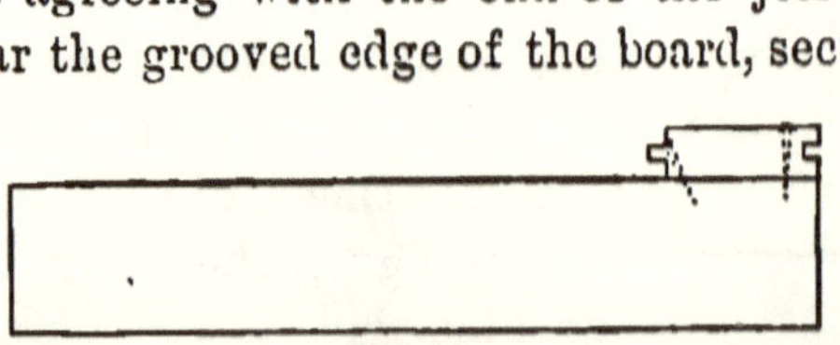

Fig. 28.

to each joist. Fig. 27 is an end view of the nailed board, while at A Fig. 31 is seen a perspective view.

Drive two nails obliquely at the base of the tongue of the board, as in Fig. 28, setting them flush by means of the brad set, thus further securing the matched board to each joist. These last two nails are said to be blinded, since the next board which is put on blinds or hides them, as in Fig. 29.

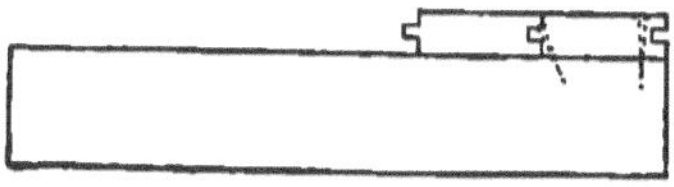

Fig. 29.

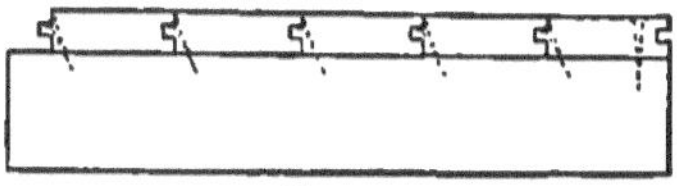

Fig. 30.

Blind nail the second board, and adding each of the remaining boards blind nail them in a similar manner, as in Fig. 30. The completed work is shown in perspective in Fig. 31.

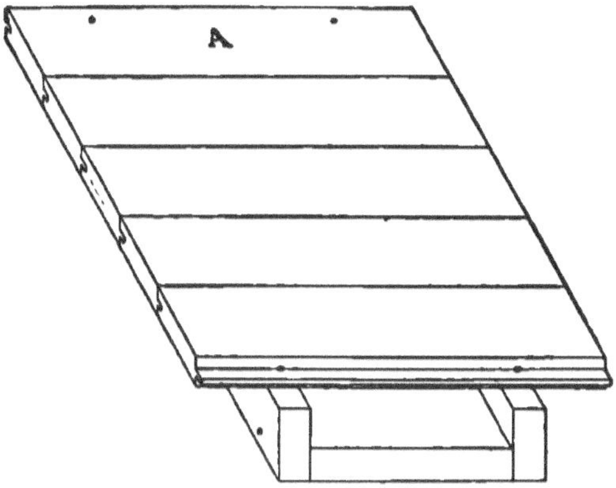

Fig. 31.

No brad heads appear in sight except the two which were perpendicularly driven near the grooved edge of the first laid matched board and the two with which the last board was secured. Rapid workmen may make two or three problems while the slowest ones are making one. Mark 5 off from 100 for every open joint between any two boards, and for every nail whose driving has caused the work to be marred.

LESSON II.

USE OF THE GAUGE.

Every board has two sides, two edges, and two ends, as in Fig. 32.

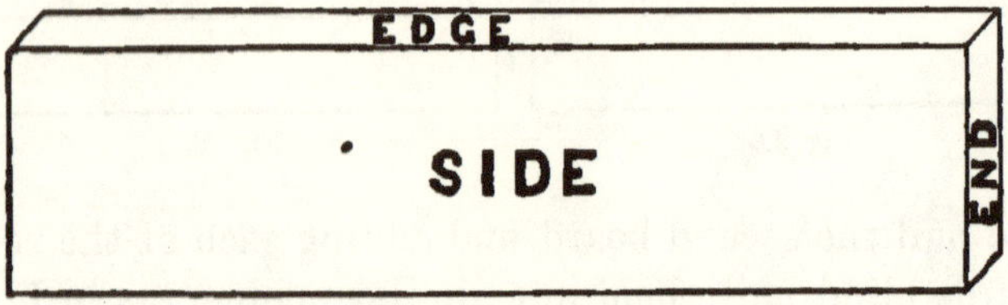

Fig. 32.

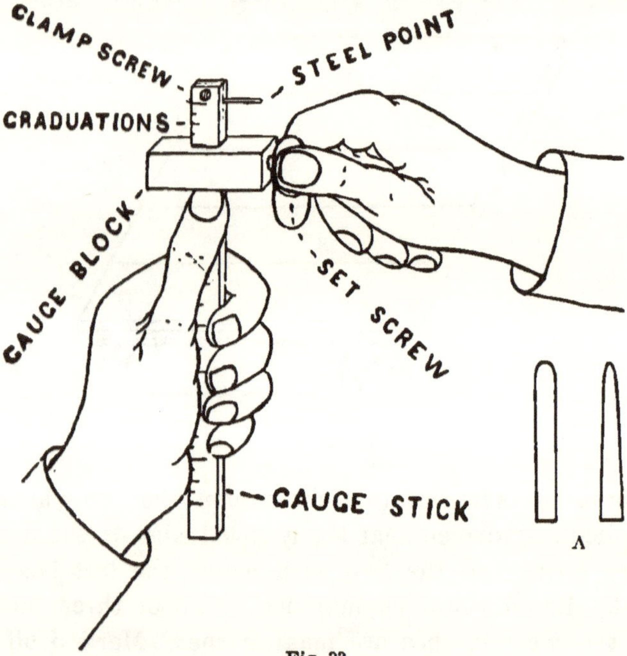

Fig. 33.

The gauge consists of two principal parts — the stick and the block, as in Fig. 33, which figure also shows the method of holding the gauge while adjusting it. (The steel point should be filed to a goose-bill shape so as to cut, not scratch, a line. See two views of it at A.)

Problem I. Gauge-Drill. — Hold the gauge-stick as in Fig. 33, the fingers of the left hand grasping it securely, while the left thumb is free to move up and down the stick, and be kept in constant contact with the block. With the right hand turn the set-screw about one-half a revolution to loosen it, then raise or lower the block, keeping hold of the set-screw meanwhile with the right hand, and keeping the left thumb meanwhile in constant contact with the block.

Requiring the observance of the above instructions, give the class a drill in unison in setting the block at inch and at half-inch graduations, then at quarter-inches, then at eighths, and finally at sixteenths.

Problem II. Gauge Practice. — For convenience in holding

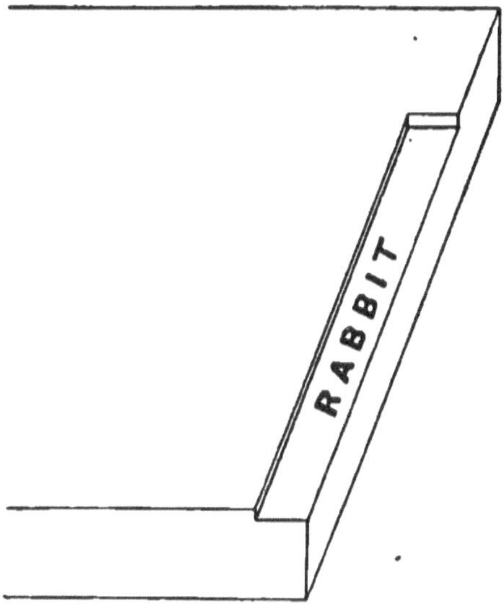

Fig. 34.

work, have a rabbit cut in the right-hand end of the bench-top, 9 in. long, 1 in. wide × $\frac{1}{8}$ in. deep, as in Fig. 34.

Provide a quantity of boards prepared by machinery, 8 in. × 2 in. × $\frac{5}{16}$ in. The thickness of $\frac{5}{16}$ in. is chosen because $\frac{7}{8}$ in. boards resawed and planed will finish to that thickness. The dimensions, 8 in. long × 2 in. wide, are chosen for convenience. The chief requisite is that the boards have straight edges. For a class of 25 pupils provide at least 100 boards. Supply each pupil with one of the above pieces. Hold it in the rabbit on the bench by means of the left hand and hold the gauge on it with the right hand, as in Fig. 35.

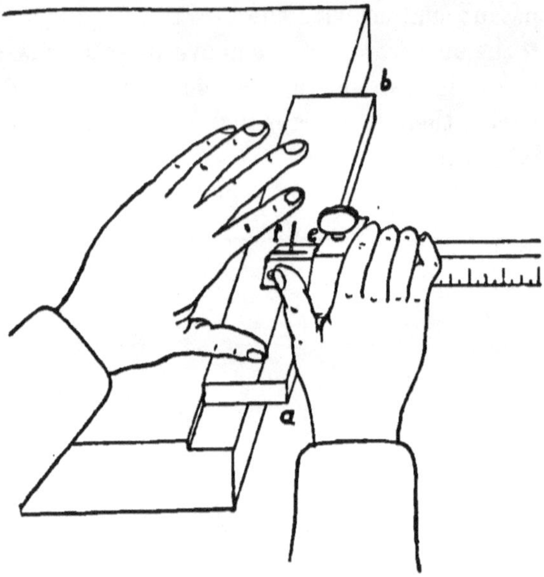

Fig. 35.

Of that portion of the gauge-stick marked *ef*, the corner which is lowest and which is farthest from you must rest on the work as in the end view, A. Fig. 36, where the steel point does not touch the wood. (*Important feature No.* 1.)

Then roll the gauge toward you till the point touches the wood, as at B. Do not roll it till the point stands vertical, as at C, for then the point will enter the wood too deeply and make too heavy a line. Skill must be obtained to make any depth of line called for by holding the gauge rolled at the

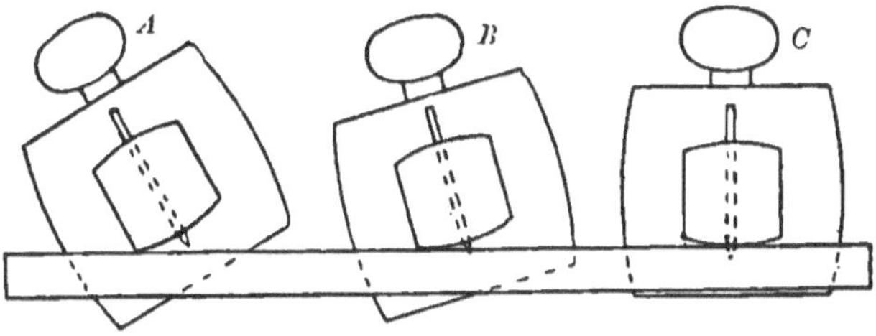

Fig. 36.

desired amount between the positions A and C. (*Important feature No. 2.*) That face of the gauge-block which rests against the edge *ab* of the work must also be placed in perfect contact throughout its entire length and kept so while a line is being gauged. (*Important feature No. 3.*) There are, therefore, three important features to be noted simultaneously in every act of gauging, and the pupil should drill till he can note them intuitively.

With the gauge set at ½ in. and observing diligently all of the above instructions gauge a line from each edge on one side of the board, as in Fig. 37. In doing this drive the gauge forward; that is, from *a* toward *b* in Fig. 35.

Fig. 37.

Repeat the process on the other side of the board, making four lines in all with the ½ in. setting. Set the gauge $\frac{7}{16}$ in.

and make four more lines as above, then set it $\frac{3}{8}$ in., or $\frac{6}{16}$ in., and repeat. So continue till $\frac{1}{16}$ in. setting is reached and a side of the board will appear as in Fig. 38.

Request each pupil to write his name neatly in the unlined space on one side of the board, and then, setting the gauge at

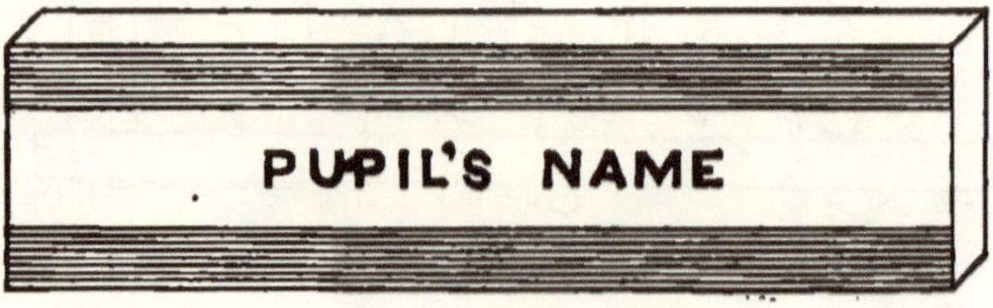

Fig. 38.

successive sixteenths above $\frac{1}{2}$ in., fill the back side with lines, as in Fig. 39. These should show improvement over the previous lines.

Fig. 39.

Rapid workmen may repeat the problem on another board. Every workman needs to master the problem as a necessary condition to his success with future lessons.

Mark 2 off from 100 for every line that is left broken or crooked.

Problem III. Gauging on Edges and Ends of Boards.— Set the gauge $\frac{1}{16}$ in. and gauge on the edges and ends of the boards used in the previous problem. Set the gauge $\frac{1}{8}$ in. and repeat. This will be found more difficult than Problem II. The work will appear as in Fig. 40.

Fig. 40.

Further practice in edge and end gauging can be had on boards which will be used in the next two lessons.

Require each pupil to write his name on every piece of finished work.

LESSON III.

MEASUREMENT.

In practical work measurement precedes gauging, which was the subject of Lesson II. In this course of lessons it is placed after gauging in order that lines may be gauged on the board used in the measurement problems.

Problem I. Measurement with Pencil.—Take a board 8 in. × 2 in. × $\frac{5}{16}$ in. Set the gauge successively at $\frac{1}{4}$ in., $\frac{1}{2}$ in., and $\frac{3}{4}$ in., and at every setting gauge two lines on *each* side

Fig. 41.

of the board. Set the gauge 1 in. and gauge one line. Each side will appear as in Fig. 41.

See that the pencil has a sharp point. This can be done by first whittling it with the knife, making a cone ¾ in. long, as

Fig. 42.

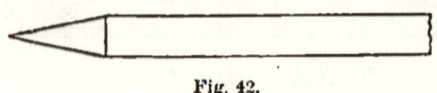

in Fig. 42, and then perfecting it with a piece of No. 0 sand-paper as follows:—

Hold the sand-paper on the bench with the left hand, as in Fig. 43. Hold the pencil-point on the sand-paper near to the end *a*, the fingers of the right hand being in the position shown at A, and draw the pencil toward *b*, rolling it underneath while doing so, bringing the fingers of the right hand

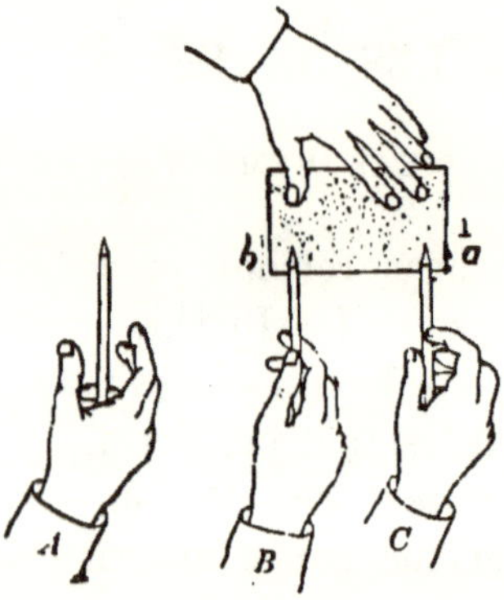

Fig. 43.

to the position shown at B, thus preserving the cone shape while sanding. Release the grasp which the thumb and the two fore-fingers have on the pencil, and, holding it by the remaining fingers, as at C, carry it back to *a* and repeat the sanding process until the pencil-point is sharp.

Hold the rule on the board, one end of it exactly agreeing

with the end of the board, and the graduated edge of the rule near to one of the gauged lines, as in Fig. 44.

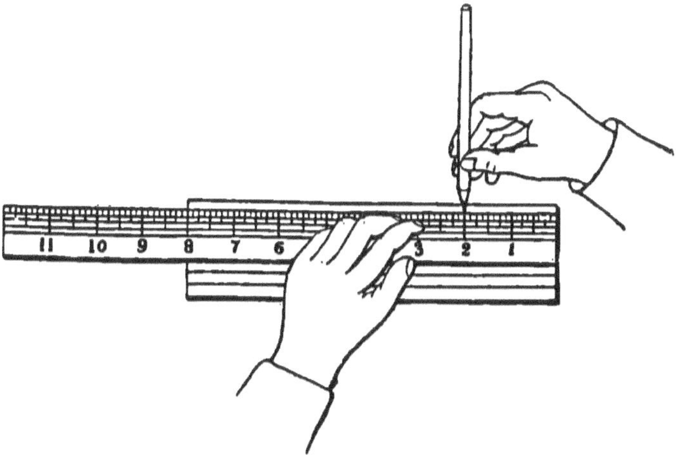

Fig. 44.

Place the pencil-point on the gauged line and successively against each $\frac{1}{2}$ in. graduation of the rule, holding it as in Fig. 44. and giving it a slight revolution to imprint a dot.

Repeat on a second line at every $\frac{1}{4}$ in., and the work will appear as in Fig. 45.

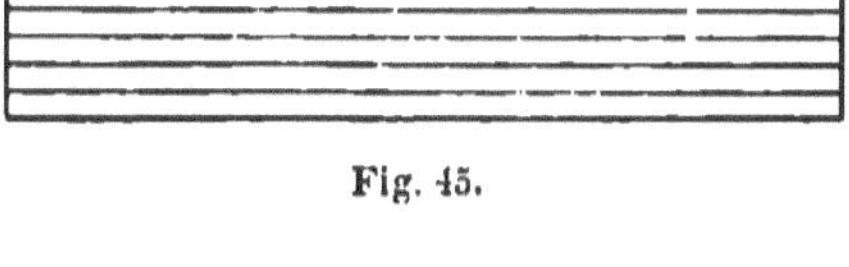

Fig. 45.

Problem II. Measurement with the Knife. — To sharpen the knife-point, first grind it till the edge is thin. This is a difficult operation, requiring skill, and a workman of experience must do it. Next put a few drops of kerosene oil on the oil stone, and hold the knife-blade on the stone, as in Fig. 46.

Fig. 46.

Fig. 47.

Keep the ground face of the blade in perfect contact with the stone, and make a few elliptical motions, as indicated by the dotted line, so adjusting the strain of the muscles in grasping the knife that the rubbing will be done at and near the edge and not at or near the back of the blade, also constantly raising and lowering the hand about ¼ in. to cause the stoning to be effective from the extreme point of the blade along the curve of the edge to the place where the blade is of full width, that is, from *c* to *d*, Fig. 47.

It is manifest that both sides of the blade need this treatment. After a few motions inspect it to see if the stoning is being done as above directed. If not, strain the muscles differently next time according as the error suggests. Test the edge by touching it to the ball of the left thumb, or by cutting a piece of soft pine. Sometimes an edge will be inadvertently ground or stoned too thin, that is, so as to leave a feather which is shown exaggerated at *a b*, Fig. 48.

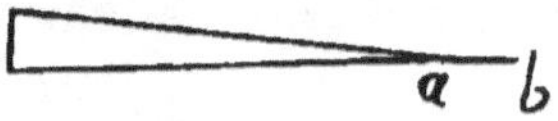

Fig. 48.

This must be worn off at *a* by light stoning or by rubbing on the palm of the hand. or on a piece of leather into which has been rubbed a little lard and emery flour, or on the clean upper of one's shoe.

Take the board used in Problem I. Hold the rule on it near the third line; hold the knife as in Fig. 49, and press it vertically, making points at every ¼ in. graduation of the rule.

See that the points made are large enough to be easily seen at arm's length, that they are of uniform size, and all at exact right angles to the gauged line.

Repeat the effort on the fourth line, placing points at every $\frac{1}{16}$ in. of alternate inches. The object of utilizing only alter-

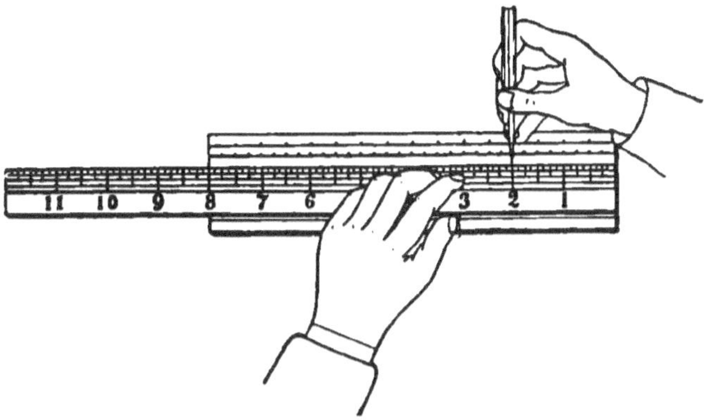

Fig. 49.

nate inches is to give opportunity to rest the hand. The work will appear as the third and fourth lines in Fig. 50.

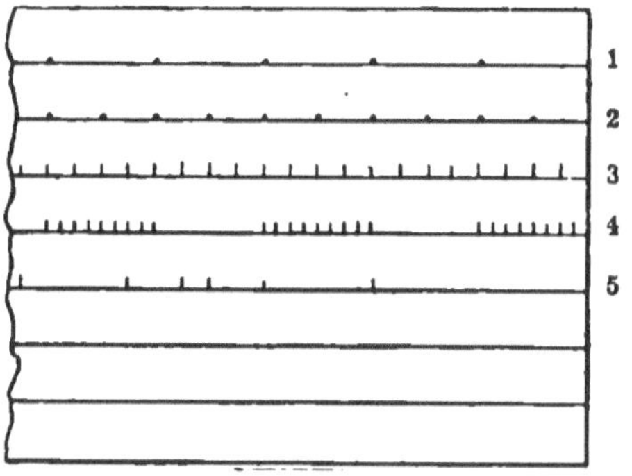

Fig. 50.

Rapid workmen may place points on additional lines. Slower workmen need not complete the sixteenths, but should do accurate work as far as they proceed.

Problem III. Varying Measurements.—Let the class work in unison, placing the rule on a fifth line and making measurements at the teacher's call. If the measurements commence at the right, and the calls are successively 1 in., $\frac{1}{2}$ in., $\frac{1}{4}$ in., $\frac{1}{8}$ in., $\frac{1}{4}$ in., $\frac{1}{2}$ in., their sum will be $2\frac{5}{8}$ in. as in the fifth line Fig. 50.

Place points on the remaining lines in a similar manner, calling a different succession of measurements for each line, until the entire class during a given effort reach the correct sum.

LESSON IV.

USE OF TRY-SQUARE AND BEVEL.

The gauge is used, as was described in Lesson II., to make lines on the side or edge of a board parallel to the grain. The try-square is used to guide a pencil or knife in making lines at right angles to the grain. It consists of two parts, the beam and the blade, as in Fig. 51.

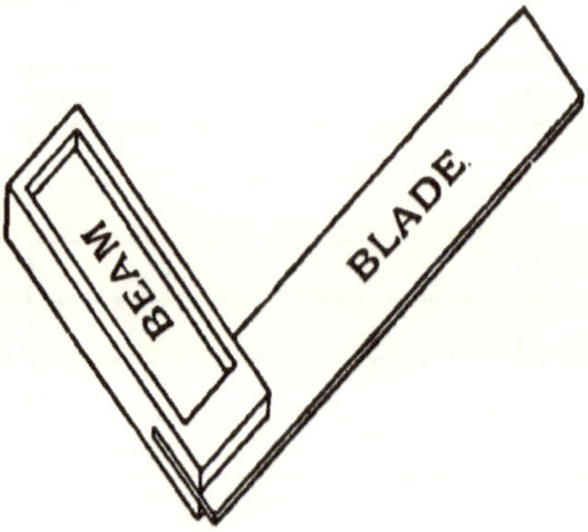

Fig. 51.

Problem I. Use of Try-Square with Pencil.—Take a board

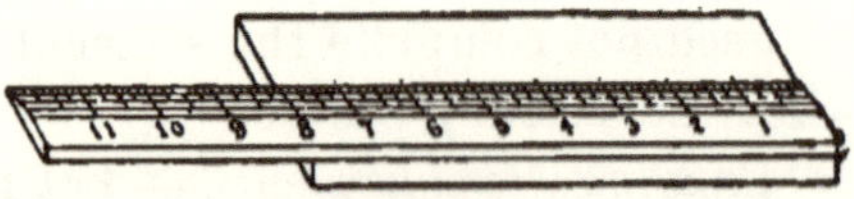

Fig. 52.

8 in. × $1\frac{1}{2}$ in. × $\frac{7}{8}$ in. Hold the rule on it, as in Fig. 52, and with a fine pencil-point, operating as in the measurement lesson, place points on the wood at every inch graduation of the rule.

Hold the try-square as in Fig. 53, using the left fore-finger to press the blade firmly to the face of the board while the thumb and remaining fingers hold the beam firmly against its edge. Place the point of the pencil in one of the points which it has made on the board, carefully move the try-square against it, raise the pencil, and with it draw a fine line across the board close to the blade of the try-square.

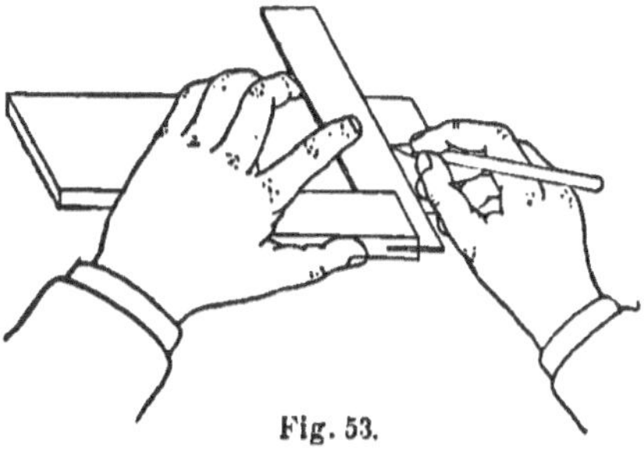

Fig. 53.

Fig. 54.

In doing this the right hand should grasp the pencil as though writing with it, and the pencil should incline to the right just enough to bring the left side of its cone of sharpening vertical, as in Fig. 54, which is a front view of the pencil, try-square blade, and board. Draw the pencil only once.

Turn the board so as to bring its front edge uppermost, and in a similar manner draw a line across that edge, as in Fig. 55.

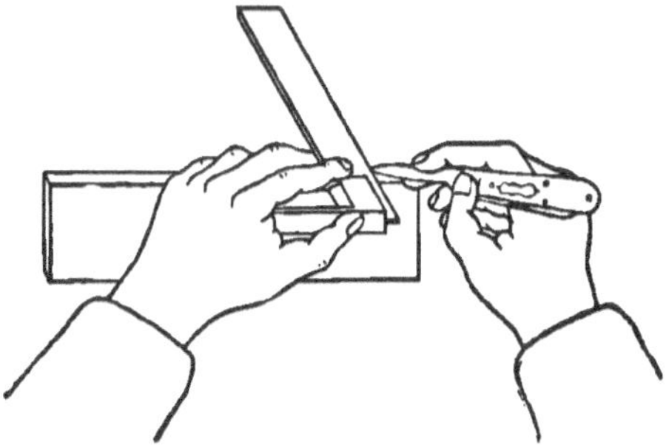

Fig. 55.

Repeat this process on the second side, and lastly on the second edge, when a line is squared entirely around the board and should meet its starting-point, as in Fig. 56.

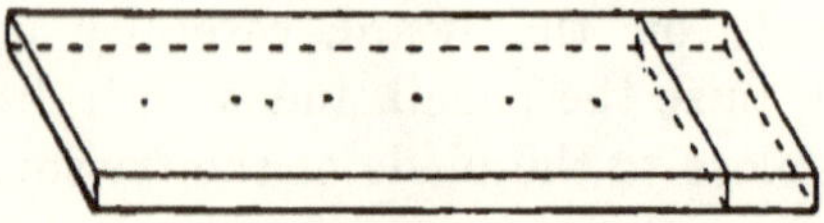

Fig. 56.

In Fig. 55 the right hand holds a knife instead of a pencil, and in that respect illustrates Problem II., instead of Problem I.

Square lines around the board through the other points. The effort of the pupil must not be to fill the board with lines, however, but to make perfect lines.

Problem II. Use of Try-Square with Knife.—Lay the rule on the board again, as in Fig. 52, and with a sharp knife point, operating as in the measurement lesson, make impressions in the wood at half-inches.

Use the knife as the pencil was used in Problem I., and square lines around the board passing through these half-inch points. The knife, like the pencil, must be inclined to the right, just enough only to allow its point to cut the wood close to the try-square blade. The knife blade must furthermore be turned as in the plan view A, Fig. 57. If it is turned too much to the right, as at B, it will move away from the try-square blade in the direction of the dotted lines. If turned too much to

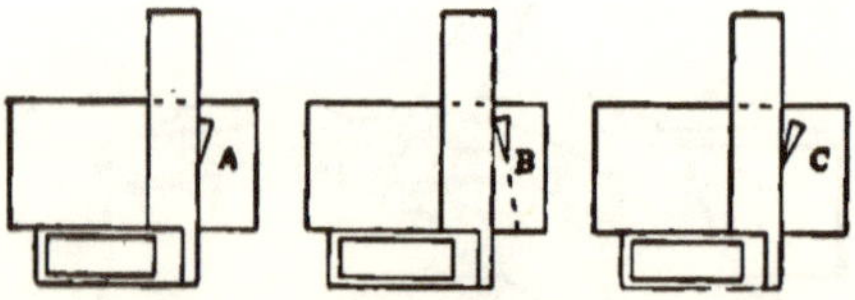

Fig. 57.

the left, as at C, it is liable to be dulled as it slides along the try-square blade, and there is danger of its pushing the try-square blade out of place, unless the grasp of the left hand is very firm. This same danger of the try-square slipping is imminent, if at any time the right hand presses the knife too hard against square.

In Problem I. instructions were given to draw the pencil but once in making any given line. This is to avoid wearing away the pencil and blurring the line. The knife, on the contrary, needs to be drawn twice, first lightly to locate the line, and second heavier to deepen it, as each line should be deep enough to be seen when held at arm's length, or should easily arrest the finger nail when drawn across it. After squaring any given line around the board, rest a few seconds before commencing another. Otherwise the muscles will tire and success be impossible. A board filled with pencil lines at every inch and knife lines at every half-inch will appear, as in Fig. 58.

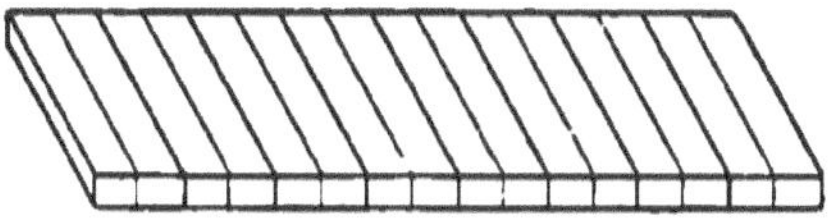

Fig. 58.

If success is not yet attained, practise the making of lines at every $\frac{1}{4}$ in., and, if necessary, at every $\frac{1}{8}$ in.

Problem III. Use of Gauge and Try-Square Combined.— Take a board 4 in. × 2 in. × $\frac{5}{16}$ in. Hold the rule on it, as in

Fig. 59.

Fig. 60.

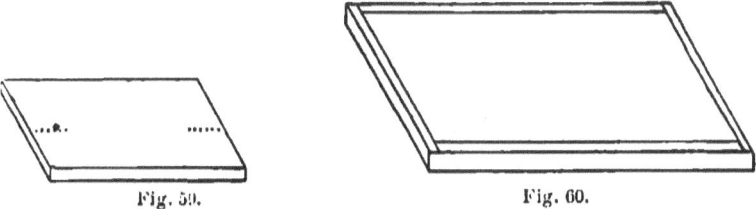

Fig. 52, and place six knife-points $\frac{1}{8}$ in. apart, measuring from each end, as in Fig. 59.

Square knife-lines through the two extreme points; set the gauge ⅛ in. and gauge from each edge of the board, starting and stopping on the squared lines, as in Fig. 60. Square knife-lines through the second points from each end, starting and stopping on the gauged lines; set the gauge ¼ in. and gauge between the knife-lines as before. Proceed in this manner till all of the twelve points are utilized, when the work will appear as in Fig. 61. Rapid workmen may draw diagonals on

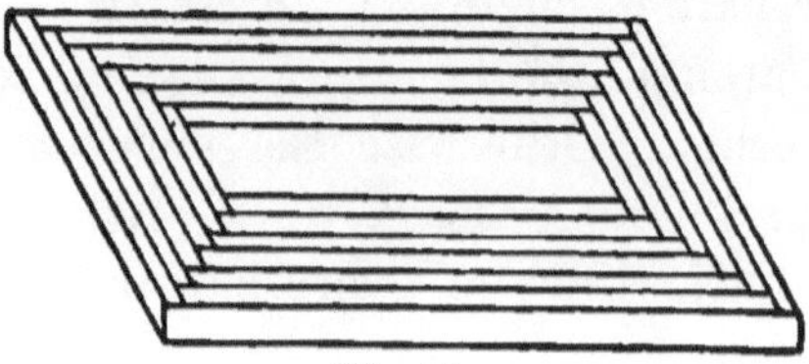

Fig. 61.

the opposite side of the board, and between them gauge lines ⅛ in. apart and square lines ¼ in. apart, as in Fig. 62.

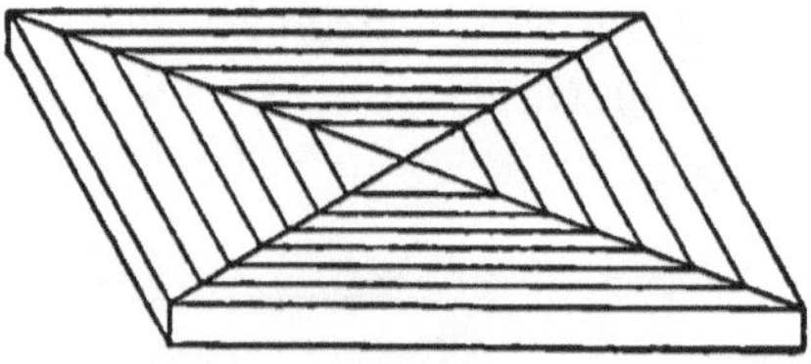

Fig. 62.

Problem IV. Use of Bevel. — In making lines other than at right angles to the edge of a board an adjustable square or bevel is needed, as in Fig. 63. It is held and used the same as the try-square.

Prepare a board, as directed in connection with Fig. 52, and through each point, with the bevel set at any chosen angle, draw pencil-lines on one side of the board. Continue these

Fig. 63.

lines around the board in a manner similar to Problem I., squaring across the edges and bevelling across the opposite side. The work will appear as in Fig. 64.

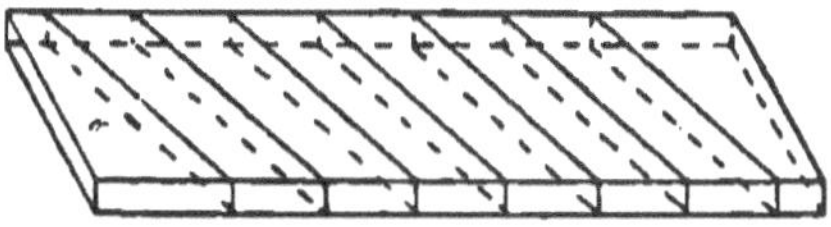

Fig. 64.

Problem V. Use of Bevel with Knife. — Place knife-points on the board at half-inches and cut bevelled lines through them, continuing them around the board like the pencil-lines. Repeat at $\frac{1}{4}$ in. if necessary.

Problem VI. Let rapid workmen take a new board and draw lines around it, using the bevel on both sides and both edges. The work will appear as in Fig. 65.

It will be a sufficient register of a pupil's attainment to inspect the work represented by Fig. 61, and mark 1 off from

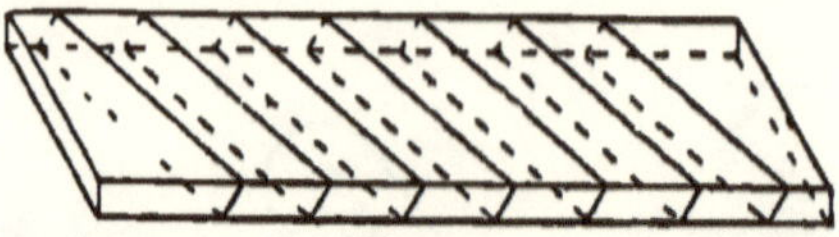

Fig. 65.

100 for every crooked line and for every line that crosses another.

LESSON V.

EXPLANATION OF THE DIFFERENCE BETWEEN SLITTING AND CUTTING-OFF SAWS.

PROVIDE for the teacher two models in wood, one of a slitting and one of a cutting-off saw. These may be each 30 in. × 3 in. × $\frac{1}{2}$ in., the slitting teeth $2\frac{1}{2}$ × $1\frac{1}{4}$, and the cutting-off teeth 2 in. × $1\frac{1}{4}$ in.

Problem I. Slitting-Saw. — Take a board 4 in. × 2 in. ×

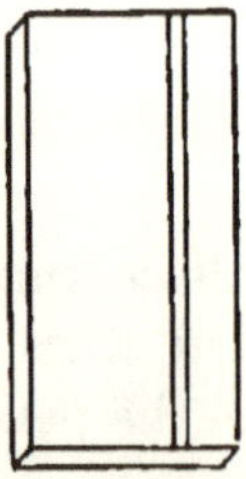

Fig. 66.

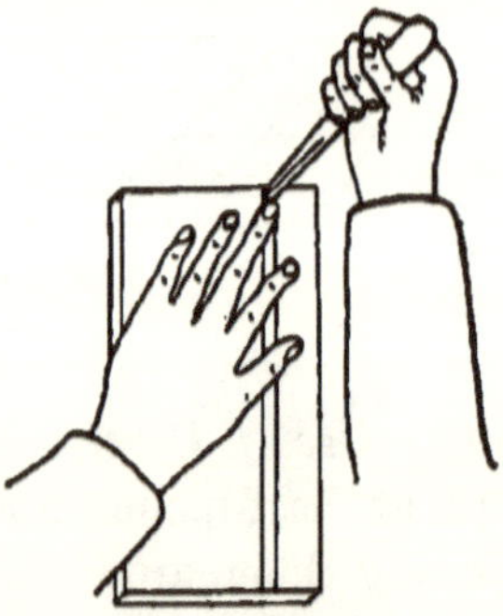

Fig. 67.

$\frac{5}{16}$ in.; on one side of it gauge two lines $\frac{1}{2}$ in. and $\frac{5}{8}$ in. respectively from one edge, as in Fig. 66.

Place the chipping-block on the bench and lay the board on it with an end toward you, guiding the chisel-edge with a finger of the left hand. Hold the $\frac{1}{8}$ in. chisel in the right hand exactly vertical, as in Fig. 67, with the bevelled edge away from you, and cut between the gauged lines a chip about $\frac{1}{16}$ in. long and entirely through the board from its upper to its lower side, as in Fig. 68.

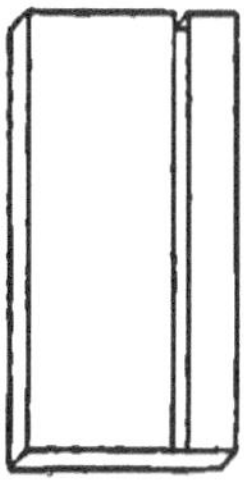
Fig. 68.

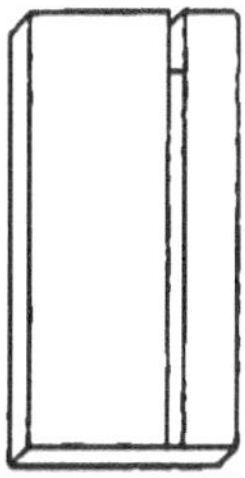
Fig. 69.

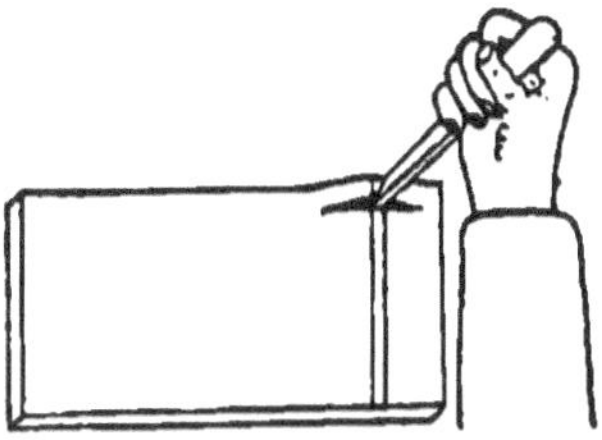
Fig. 70.

Continue in this manner to cut successive chips, each about $\frac{1}{16}$ in. long, and each entirely through the thickness of the board, until the slowest workmen have made a cutting about $\frac{1}{2}$ in. long, as in Fig. 69. This cutting is called a kerf.

Rapid workmen will have made a kerf nearly or quite the length of the board.

If we should make two lines crosswise of the board and endeavor to chisel between them, we could not make a kerf, but should splinter the board, as in Fig. 70.

Fig. 71.

Fig. 71 is a view of the wooden model of a slitting-saw.

Its teeth are a succession of chisels. The front edge of each tooth, as *a b*, is at right angles to a line touching the points, and all of the slant of the tooth is on the rear edge, as *a c.* From the above experimental problem it is manifest that such a saw is suitable for slit-sawing only.

Problem II. Cutting-off Saw. — Take the board used in the previous problem, or one similar to it, and using try-square and knife, make two lines across the board $\frac{1}{16}$ in. apart, the right hand line being $\frac{1}{2}$ in. from the end, as in Fig. 72.

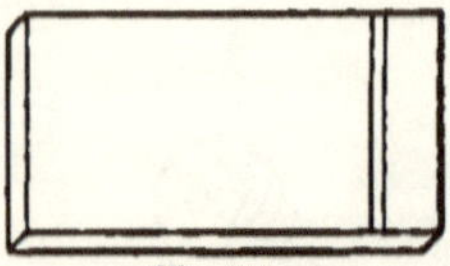

Fig. 72.

Lay the board on the chipping-block, holding it with the left hand. Hold the knife as a pen is held in writing. Incline it toward you about 30° from a vertical position, as in Fig. 73, but do not incline it at all toward the right or left.

Draw the knife across the board along one of the above lines, and then along the other. Continue to do this alternately, and what happens? "The wood splits out between the lines, making a kerf." If we proceed in this manner, the board will soon be cut in two.

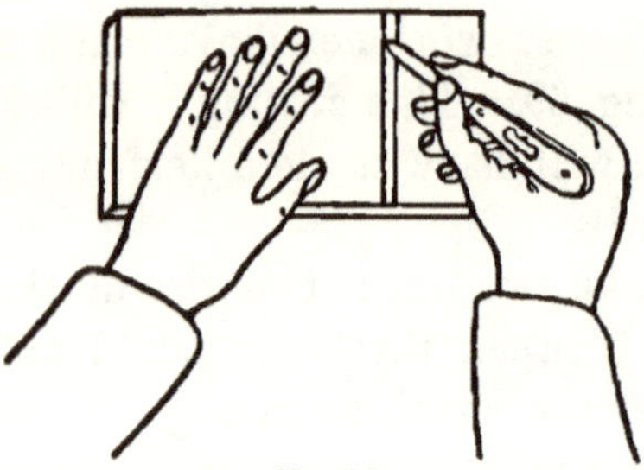

Fig. 73.

A kerf cannot be cut lengthwise of the grain by this process, because the wood will not split out between the lines.

If we had a knife with two blades of equal length and $\frac{1}{16}$ in. apart, we could draw it through both lines at the same time.

Fig. 74 is a view of the wooden model of a cutting-off saw. Its teeth slant about equally on each edge and are bevelled so that alternate teeth are pointed on one side of the saw, the intervening teeth being pointed on the other side.

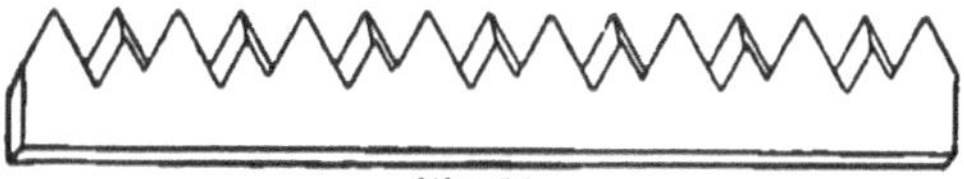

Fig. 74.

Its use produces a result quite similar to the above experimental problem with the knife; that is, marking two parallel lines across the board and breaking out the wood between them. The teeth of a cutting-off saw may then be considered as a succession of pairs of knife-points.

Another important fact concerning saws is that the teeth are "set;" that is, alternate teeth bent toward one side, and the intervening teeth bent toward the other side. In the cutting-off saw the teeth which are pointed on a given side are bent toward that side, as in Fig. 75.

Fig. 75.

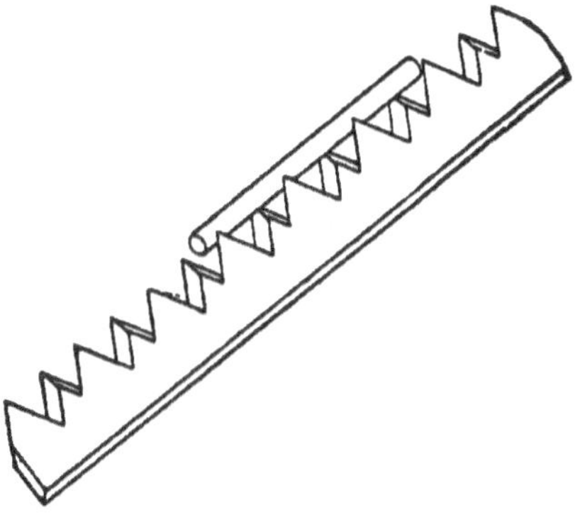

Fig. 76.

The object of this is to have the saw cut a kerf wider than the thickness of its blade, in order that the saw may pass easily through the kerf which it is making. Owing to this setting and to its bevelled filing, a cutting-off saw appears grooved along the line of teeth when viewed endwise, as in Fig. 75. Hold the model inclined, as in Fig. 76, and a straight rod 10 in. long × ¼ in. diameter will slide down this groove. An ordinary needle will slide down the teeth of a cutting-off saw in a similar manner.

Each pupil may take in hand the two 18-in. saws on his bench, examine them carefully, and hold the slitting-saw in his right hand and the cutting-off saw in his left.

Very few pupils will fail to make the selection accurately after the above experimental description.

LESSON VI.

USE OF SAWS.

Problem I. To Start the Kerf. — Take a waste piece of board of any dimensions, 4 × 2 × ⅞ will answer. Place it

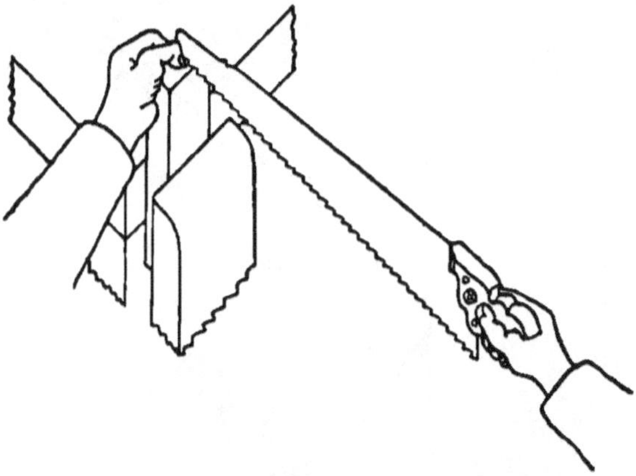

Fig. 77.

end uppermost in the vise. With try-square and pencil draw lines on the upper end ¼ in. apart. Hold the slitting-saw in the right hand, guiding it with the left thumb so that its teeth shall rest on one of the lines. Drive the saw *first forward* and then back several times, taking full length strokes to within about 1 in. of each end, meantime so controlling the muscles of the right hand that, although the saw teeth touch the wood during each entire stroke, they shall not cut into it *at all.* The commencement of this process is illustrated in Fig. 77.

The teacher should be able to drive the saw forward and back on the left hand, as in Fig. 78, touching the palm con-

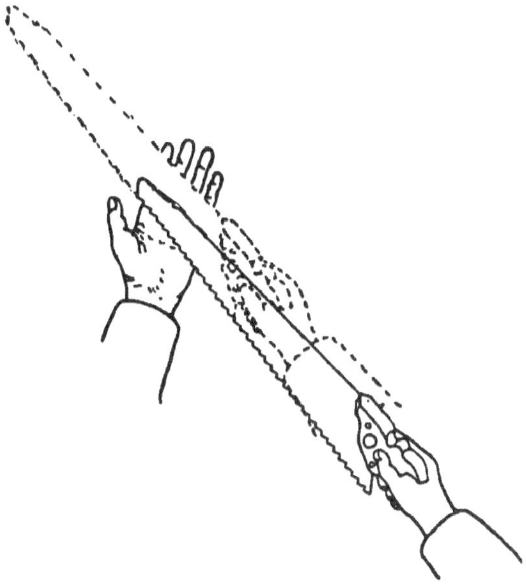

Fig. 78.

stantly, but not injuring it, to illustrate clearly to pupils that it can be done. Require the class to drive the saw forward and back on the wood as above, acting in concert as the teacher counts 1, 2; 1, 2, etc., in order to get a moderate, regular motion, as boys left to themselves will saw with fury. The power to follow all of the above directions we will term getting command of the saw; and every pupil needs to get this command before being allowed to saw.

Next let the weight of the saw bear on the board while the forward stroke is being made, but not during the backward stroke, and the saw will descend into the wood, making a cut which is technically called a kerf.

At the commencement and close of each forward stroke the saw should be held at command. Midway of each forward stroke it should do its heaviest cutting. The full stroke should be a crescendo, followed by a diminuendo as in music. The saw should be held at command during the entire backward stroke.

Problem II. Slit-Sawing Near to Line. — Take a board 8 in. × 2 in. × $\frac{7}{8}$ in. and make an × on one edge. Set the gauge $\frac{1}{4}$ in. and gauge two lines on each side and each end, as in Fig. 79. Set the gauge $\frac{1}{2}$ in. and repeat; then $\frac{3}{4}$ in. and

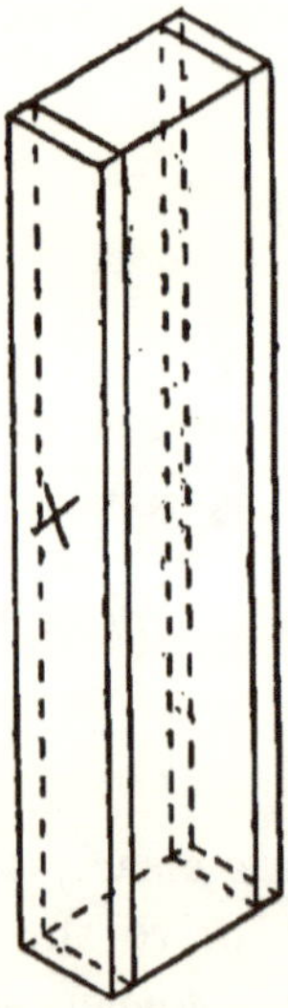

Fig. 79.

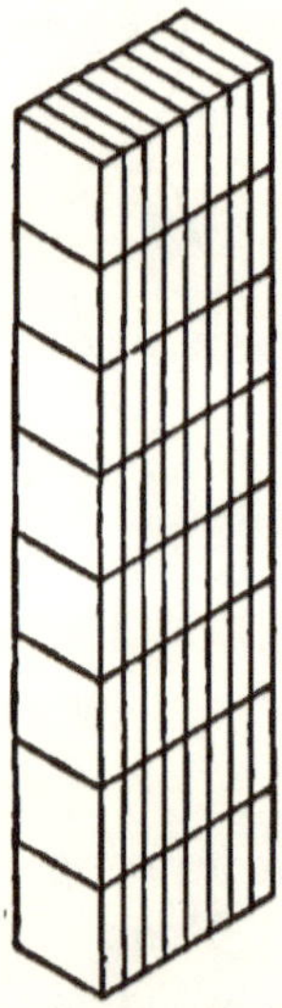

Fig. 80.

repeat; then 1 in. and gauge around once, that is, from the × edge. Square around with fine pencil-point at every inch. The work will appear as in Fig. 80.

Hold the work in the vise, end uppermost, as in Fig. 77, one-half of it buried, and saw a kerf $\frac{1}{16}$ in. to the right of the right-hand line. When this kerf has proceeded downward 1 in., that is, to the first squared line, stop and examine it carefully, and if it has not kept parallel with the gauged line, scrape it with that portion of the saw nearest the handle, commonly called the heel of the saw, until it is restored to parallel. A, Fig. 81, represents a kerf at first running to the

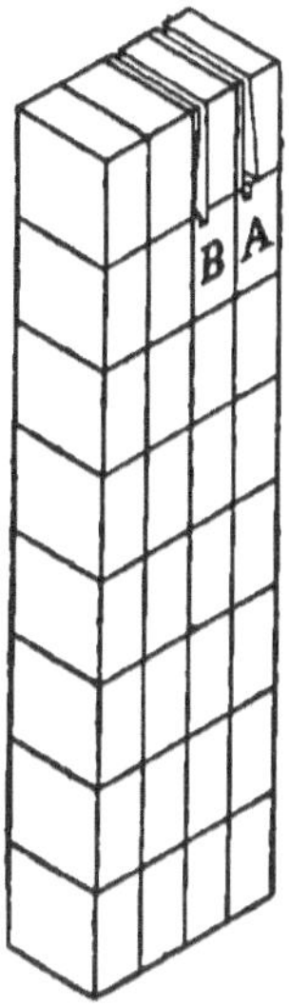

Fig. 81.

Fig. 82.

right, but afterwards restored to its proper position and continued a little below the squared line. B represents a kerf running at first to the left and afterward restored. On no account should the kerf be allowed to proceed below the squared line till its wrong direction, if it have any, is rectified, and the aim of the pupil must be to keep the saw from running at all to either side. Furthermore, the location of the kerf should be as accurate on the back side of the work as on the front.

Proceed to saw down to the second squared line, stop and

inspect, and correct if necessary. Proceed to saw down to the third squared line, and stop on it.

In the same manner saw near to the remaining gauged lines. The work will appear as the upper portion of Fig. 82, where for clearness, as also in Fig. 81, only one-half of the number of lines gauged on Fig. 80 are shown. Mark 10 off from 100 for every line which at its finish deviates $\frac{1}{16}$ in. from its proper position.

Problem III. Slit-Sawing Close to Line.—Place the opposite end of the work uppermost, and saw so that the left side of the saw-blade shall cut to the centre of the line, observing in all other respects the directions given above, and the work will appear as the lower portion of Fig. 82.

Problem IV. Cut-off Sawing Near to Line.—Take a board 8 in. × $3\frac{1}{2}$ in. × $\frac{7}{8}$ in., gauge-lines at every $\frac{1}{2}$ in. on the sides and square pencil-lines round at every $\frac{1}{2}$ in. Put it in the vise with an edge uppermost, and, observing directions given in Problem II., saw near to every line, as in the upper portion of Fig. 83.

Mark 5 off from 100 for every line that deviates, at its finish, $\frac{1}{16}$ in. from its proper position.

Problem V. Cut-off Sawing Close to Line.—Place the board in the vise with the opposite edge uppermost, and, observing directions given in Problem III., saw close to the line. The work will appear as in the lower portion of Fig. 83.

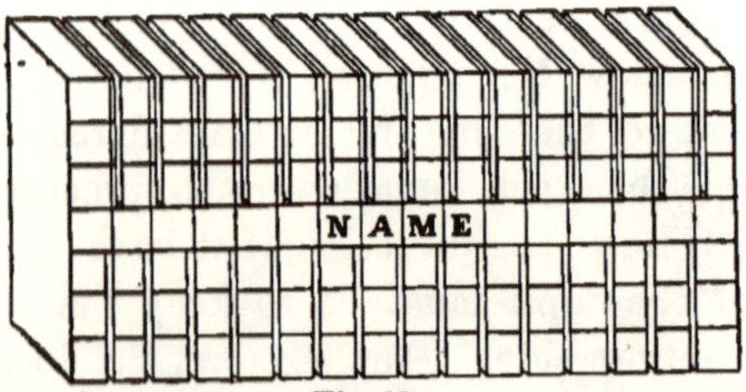

Fig. 83.

Rapid workmen may take a second board and repeat, which repetition will increase their proficiency, or they may saw diagonally.

LESSON VII.

SURFACE PLANING.

The two sides of a board, or the four sides of a square stick, being larger surfaces than edges or ends, are often technically called surfaces, and planing them is known as surface planing.

The principal planes used by wood workmen are jack-plane 14 in. long, fore-plane 14 in.. jointer 22 in., smooth-plane 8 in., and block-plane 6 in., and these may be of wood or of iron. The blade of the jack-plane is ground so that its edge is a continuous curve, as in Fig. 84. All other plane blades are ground as in Fig. 85; that is, with the edge straight for some-

Fig. 84.

Fig. 85.

what more than one-half of its length, then rounded slightly at each end. The jack-plane and block-plane each have single blades, as in Fig. 86. All others have double blades; that is, the blade is provided with a cap, as in Fig. 87.

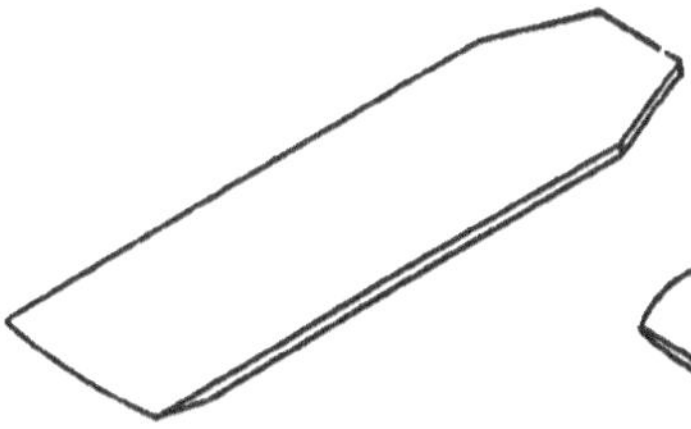

Fig. 86.

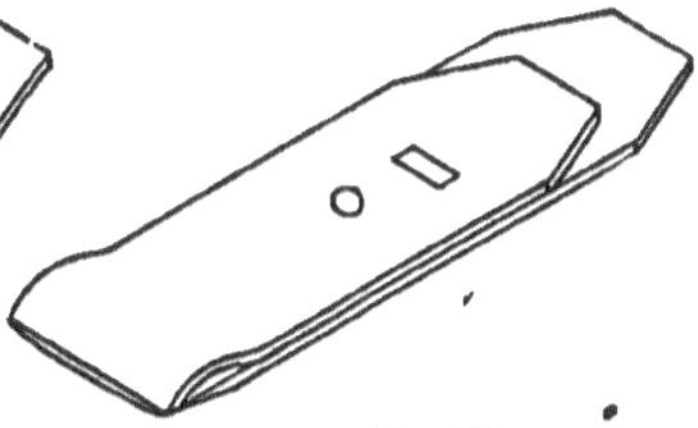

Fig. 87.

This cap is necessary when cross-grained or complex-grained boards are to be planed. It is then brought down as near to the cutting-edge of the blade as possible, but for straight-grained wood it is of no special service, and had better be set back about $\frac{1}{32}$ in. It is so set in these lessons.

Only three planes are needed in this series of lessons, to the first two of which we will for convenience give special names of our own. An 8 in. wooden smooth-plane (Fig. 88) is used for all rough planing, and we will call it the *roughing-plane.* An 8 in. iron smooth-plane (Fig. 89) is used for all finish

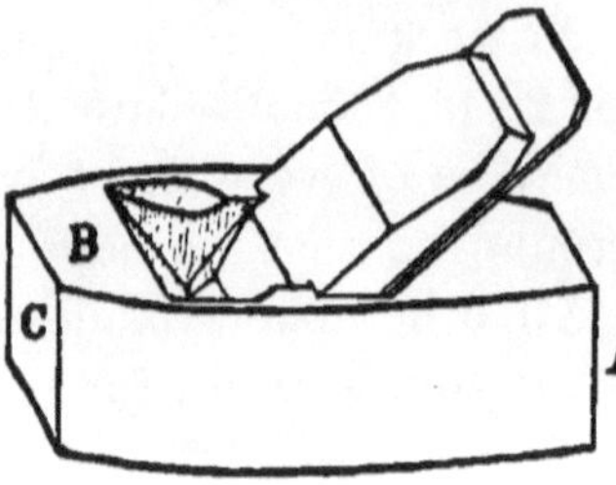

Fig. 88.

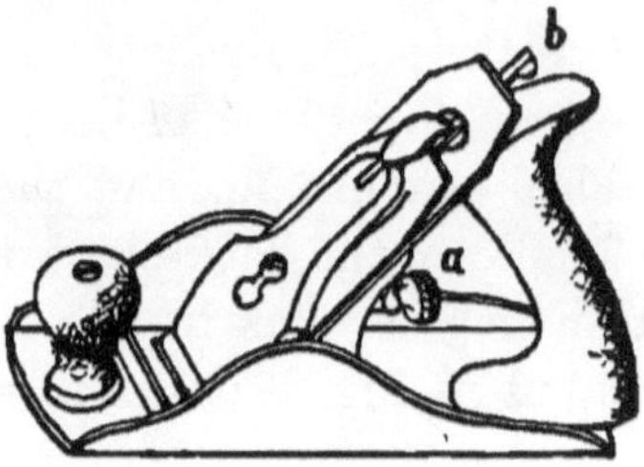

Fig. 89.

planing parallel with the grain; that is, on sides and edges of boards, and we will call it the *finishing-plane.* A 6 in. iron *block-plane* (Fig. 90) is used for all planing on the ends of boards.

The block-plane differs from all others in having its blade inverted, as in Fig. 91, and is set at a more acute angle with the face or under side of the block, as will be seen in comparing Fig. 90 with Figs. 88 and 89.

The knob on the front end of the block-plane seen at A Fig. 90 is a screw to hold in place the throat-plate which is

A

Fig. 90.

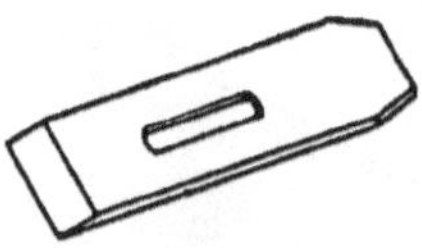

Fig. 91

the adjustable front portion of the face or under side of the plane. Sometimes this throat-plate is accidentally slipped till it strikes the blade, and the throat is thereby closed so that shavings cannot come out. Look out for this danger.

Problem I. Rough Planing. — Each pupil takes his roughing-plane in hand and follows instructions given by the teacher, who shows how to hold the plane while removing the blade, and then names and explains each of its parts. In removing the blade, strike with a hammer either on the rear end, A, or on the front portion of the top, B, but never on the front end, C. Re-assemble and adjust the parts.

Take a board, preferably 12 in. wide, though any other width will answer, and saw off for each pupil a piece 8½ in. long. With pencil and straight-edge draw lines on it lengthwise 3 in. apart, as in Fig. 92.

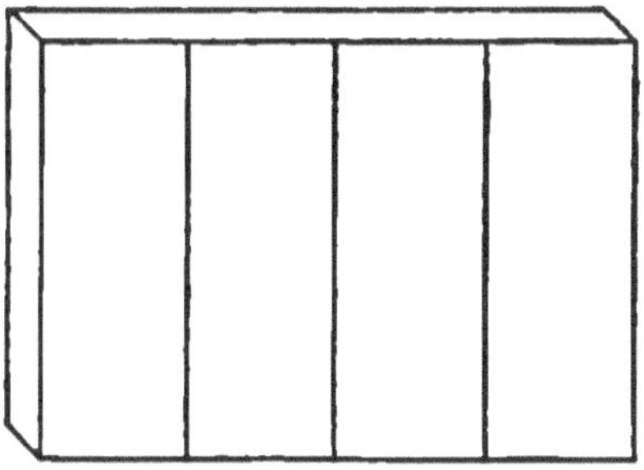

Fig. 92.

Fig. 93.

Hold this piece in the vise and saw *on* the lines, dividing it in four pieces, 3 in. rough width. Hold these pieces in the vise successively and rough-plane both edges till saw marks are removed. Two or three strokes of the roughing-plane ought to do this. Be sure that the plane cuts a shaving at every stroke and that it cuts a shaving along the entire length of the work. A common fault with beginners is to omit planing at the rear end, or the end first met by the blade, and commencing when the blade is well on the wood continue to plane the rest of the way, giving the board the tapering shape of Fig. 93. Make sure at the outset that this tendency is overcome.

Problem II. Surface Planing. — Take the finishing-plane apart, give names to the several pieces, and explain the province of each. Re-assemble the plane and adjust it thus: Holding it with face uppermost, sight along the face to see if the blade projects. Turn the adjusting-screw, *a*, in the necessary direction, and move the lever, *b*, the necessary way to cause the middle portion of the blade's edge to appear in sight while its ends do not, as in the diagram Fig. 94.

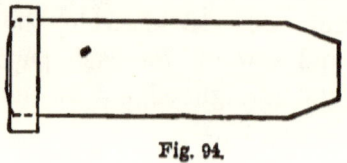

Fig. 94.

Put on the blackboard, or on cardboard to hang permanently on the wall, the two diagrams Fig. 95, to assist pupils

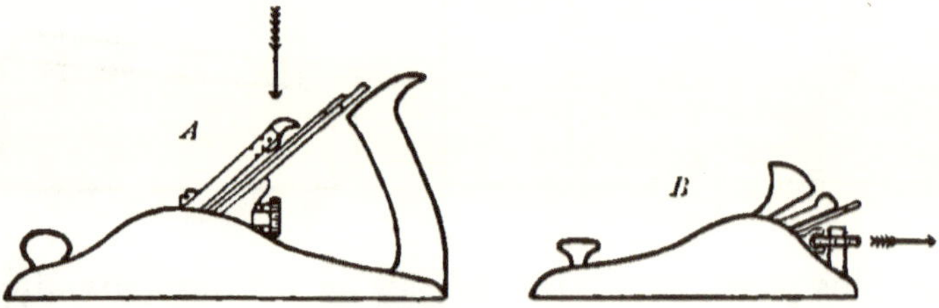

Fig. 95.

in knowing which way to turn adjusting-screws. A is a diagram of the finishing-plane, B of the block-plane. To force the blade of either plane downward, that is, when a thicker shaving is needed, turn the front side of the adjusting-screw in the direction of the arrow. To draw the blade up turn the screw in the opposite direction.

A good way for beginners to test the adjustment minutely is to hold the plane in the left hand, face uppermost, and with the right hand draw a small strip of thin board (4 in. × 1 in.

× ¼ in. will answer) over the edge. A shaving should be cut when drawing such a strip along the middle of the plane's face, as on the dotted line, *a*, Fig. 96, but not when drawing it near the edge, as on either of the dotted lines *b* or *c*.

Fig. 96.

Take one of the pieces which were sawed from Fig. 92, and whose edges have been rough planed, hold it on the top of the bench against the planing pin, and *clean* one of its sides with the finishing plane, thus: —

Suppose three lines to be drawn lengthwise on the board dividing the side in four sections, as in Fig. 97. First drive the plane so as to have the middle of its blade cut along the

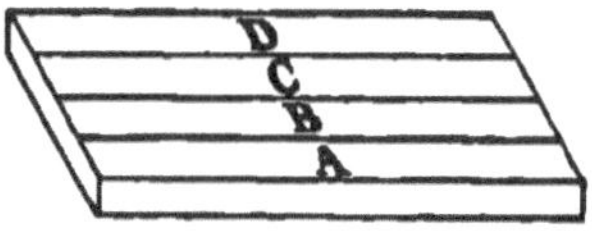

Fig. 97.

middle of section A, then along the middle of section B, then C, and lastly D.

It is possible that this effort to plane may demonstrate that some farther slight movements of the screw, *a*, and lever, *b*, Fig. 89, are necessary, as the middle line of the shaving ought to come from the middle point of the blade's edge.

The side of the board ought now to be clean. If it is not, repeat with four more sectional shavings when it certainly should be. Do not plane with fury and without thought, or waste the wood, as in Fig. 93.

Clean the opposite side of the board in like manner.

Next *true* the first side, thus: Provide each pupil with a straight edge which may be of soft wood 16 in. × 2 in. × $\frac{3}{16}$ in. with both edges carefully straightened and parallel. Test the work with this straight edge in eight places; viz., three lengthwise tests, one near each edge and one along the middle, as on the dotted lines, Fig. 98; three crosswise tests, one near each end and one across the middle, as on the dotted lines, Fig. 99, and two diagonal tests, as in Fig. 100.

Fig. 98.

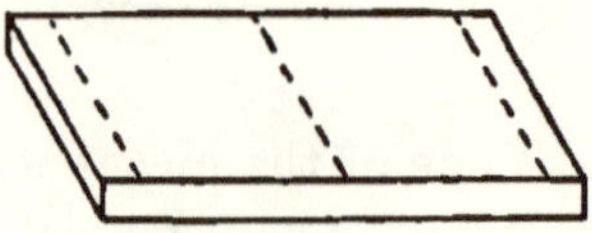

Fig. 99.

Plane wherever these eight tests show the surface to be high, or, in other words, plane the whole surface, following the directions above given for cleaning the surface, with the exception of omitting to plane such points as the above eight tests show to be low. This may be difficult at first, but the difficulty must be mastered. Write pupil's name on the first side when thus trued.

True the opposite side of the board in like manner. If facility has been promptly acquired, the two sides will be parallel, since they were mill planed parallel before the pupil took them. If the pupil has disturbed their parallelism, it must be restored by setting the gauge to the thinnest corner, then gauging *from* the first side on both edges and both ends and planing to gauge-lines.

Treat all four of the boards in like manner. Rapid workmen will complete the four, and perhaps more, while slower workmen are completing one or two.

When one of the diagonal tests of Fig. 100 shows the board to be high in the middle and the other one shows it to be high in the corners, the surface is said to be "winding," and the process of planing it true is called "taking out the wind." To test long boards for windage, such as two feet and over, apply two straight edges, each ⅞ in. thick × 2 in. wide, one near each end, and sight across the top, as in Fig. 101.

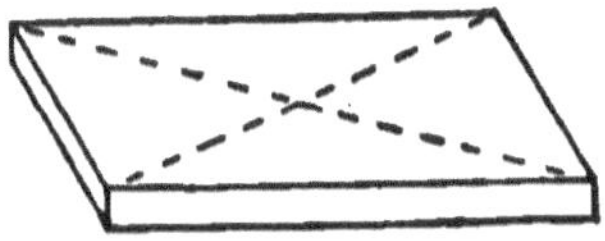

Fig. 100.

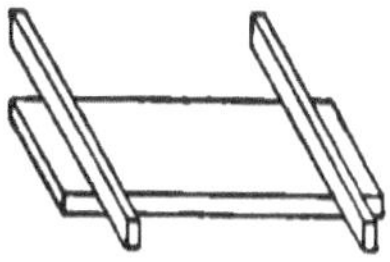

Fig. 101.

Notice that in this problem we have performed two operations, first cleaning the surface and second truing it. In the first operation the plane may be set somewhat coarser than in the second, but in both it should be set as fine as the work to be done will allow. The grinding and oil-stoning must at present be done by the teacher or by some one with skill to do it.

If a board to be planed is wider or narrower than 3 in., more or less than the four sections mentioned in connection with Fig. 97 will be needed. Also the width and consequent number of these sections will be affected by the length of straight portion of the edge of the plane blade.

LESSON VIII.

EDGE AND END PLANING.

IN mechanics, as in arithmetic, there are four fundamental rules, one or more of which are practised in every problem, and no workman can become a skilful operator without understanding and mastering them. They are as follows:—

Rule I. Measure accurately according to plan.

Rule II. Make perfect lines.

Rule III. Cut rapidly near to lines.

Rule IV. Cut carefully exactly to lines.

The present lesson illustrates these rules clearly.

As in arithmetic, multiplication is really a short method of performing uniform addition, and division a short method of performing uniform subtraction, and thus the four rules can be considered analytically as two; so in mechanics the above first two rules may be condensed into the statement: *Lay out work accurately,* and the last two into the statement: *Work to lines.*

Problem I. Edge-Planing. — Hold in the vise one of the boards which were surface planed in Lesson VII., and use the finishing-plane (Fig. 89, Lesson VII.) to true one edge, thus: —

Imagine a line to be drawn along the middle of the edge, as in Fig. 102, dividing the edge in two sections, A and B.

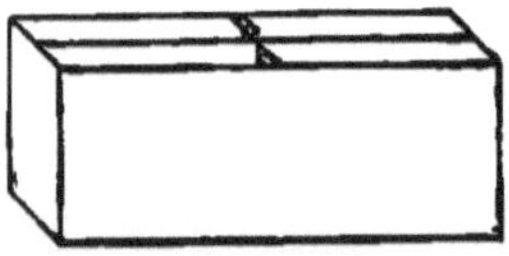

Fig. 102.

Fig. 103.

To insure driving the plane so that the middle point of its cutting-edge shall glide along the middle of section A, guide it with the fingers of the left hand, as in Fig. 103. In this guiding the left fingers are held under the plane and in contact with the wood as the plane glides along.

Take a similar shaving from section B, and a third one along the middle of the edge, imaging no line on it.

Test the work with straight-edge lengthwise in three places, as in Fig. 98, Lesson VII., and with try-square crosswise in three places, as in Fig. 104 below, and plane where these tests show the face to be high. Remember the blade of the plane *must* be kept properly adjusted, and set as fine as will do the work required.

A plane should never be driven over a board unless it cuts, as that will dull it more than the process of cutting, and a blade edge should never rest on the board when the plane is being drawn back, as that also will dull it.

Place a tried mark, as in Fig. 105, on the first side and first edge finished, enclosing their common corner. This side and this edge are to be worked from in all future laying out.

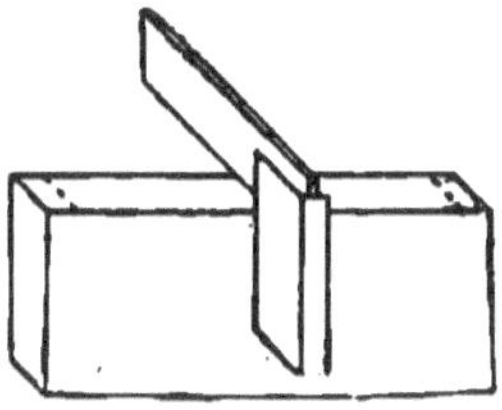

Fig. 104.

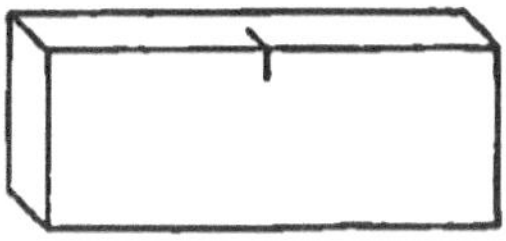

Fig. 105.

To finish the second edge set the gauge $2\frac{3}{4}$ in., *Rule I.;* gauge *on* both sides *from* the finished edge, *Rule II.;* plane away the surplus wood till the lines are nearly reached, using the roughing-plane, *Rule III.;* and then plane exactly to the lines, using the finishing-plane, *Rule IV.* Test with try-square just before reaching the lines, and complete the planing as its tests suggest, but *do not on any account plane below the lines,* even though the edge is not perfectly square with the side. It will be square, however, if skill is acquired to make it so just before reaching the lines, and then to keep it so as the lines are reached.

Plane all four of the boards in like manner. Rapid workmen will finish the four boards, and perhaps make one or two more, while slower workmen are making one or two only.

Problem II. End-Planing. — Take one of the boards planed in Problem I., and using the knife and try-square as in Lesson IV., square around ¼ in. from one end, as in

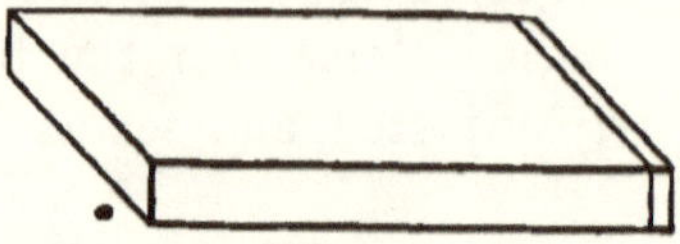

Fig. 106.

Fig. 106, *Rule II.* In doing so always place the beam of the try-square against the tried side or tried edge mentioned in connection with Fig. 105. This is to insure accurate work.

Place the board on the saw-block, as in Fig. 107, and saw very close to the lines without touching them. *Rule III.*

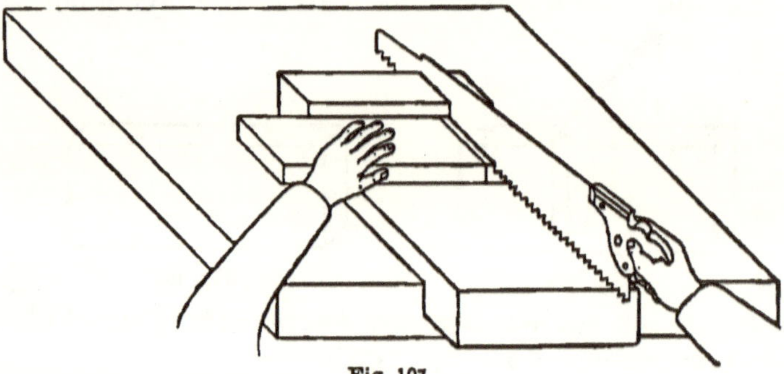

Fig. 107.

Hold the work in the vise and plane to the lines, using the block-plane as in Fig. 108, *Rule IV.* Test with try-square when nearly done so as not to plane beyond the lines.

In case it is not yet possible for a given pupil to saw sufficiently near to the lines, the wood remaining had better be chipped away, as in Fig. 109, and those who are so timid as to saw far from the line will have to chip twice, the first chipping being shown at Fig. 110.

Let us now give more detailed instruction for this chipping and planing, and explain Figs. 108 to 111 more minutely.

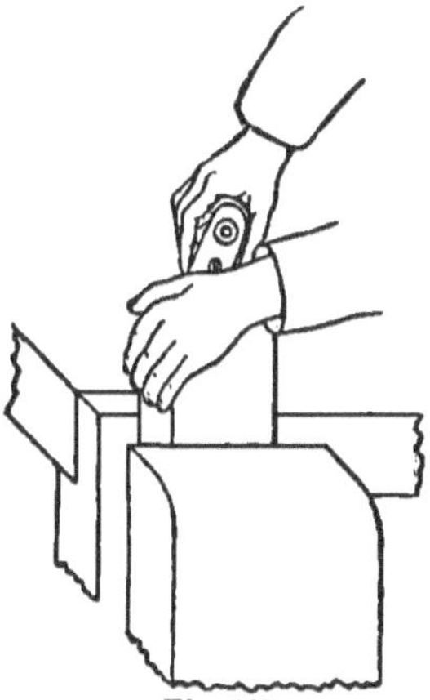

Fig. 108.

In Fig. 108 the hands nearly cover up both the plane and the work; but the intention is to show the palm of the left

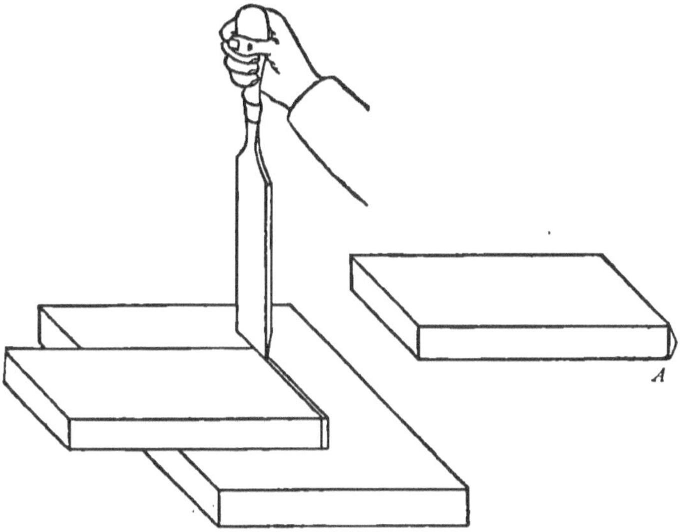

Fig. 109.

hand resting on the knob or throat plate screw of the plane, while the left fingers rest against the edge of the work farthest from the workman, and thus while assisting the right hand to drive the plane, give the workman power to stop the plane at will.

In Fig. 109 the work is represented lying on a chipping-block. Use the 1 in. chisel, utilizing not more than one-third to one-half of its edge at a stroke, as shown in the figure. The unutilized portion of the edge will, at each stroke after the first, follow the cut made by the preceding stroke and so guide the chisel. Let the chisel start in the line, and cut a surface slanting a little to the right so as not to disturb the line on the opposite side of the board. Turn the board over and cut from the line on that side in like manner, when the end will be crowning, or roof shaped, as seen, exaggerated, at A. Place the board in the vise, and, operating as in Fig. 108, plane off this crowning portion exactly to the lines. This chiselling and planing may be called a triple application of Rule IV.

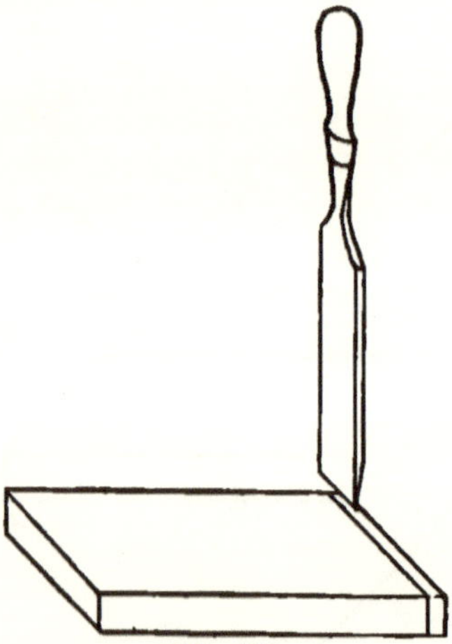

Fig. 110.

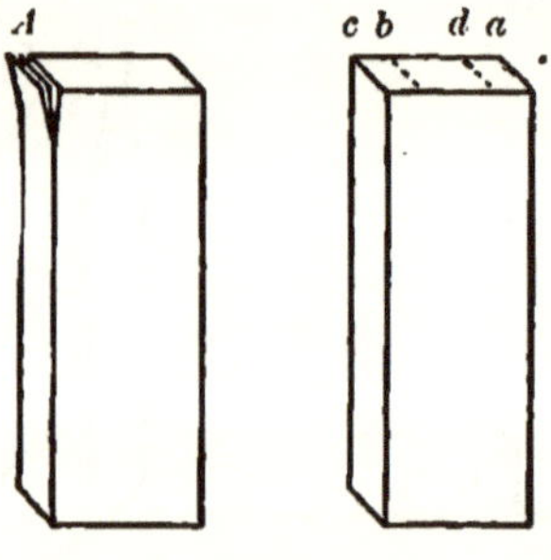

Fig. 111.

In Fig. 110 use only from one-third to one-half of the chisel-edge at a stroke, as was done in Fig. 109. Chip vertically, and proceed entirely across the board, keeping about $\frac{1}{32}$ in. from the line. The work is then ready to fully treat, as in Fig. 109. A skilful pupil will saw close to the line, and to such these clipping directions are unnecessary in this connection.

Sometimes the amount of wood outside of the lines is too little to saw, and would then better be chipped away, instead, in accordance with Fig. 110, making one cut about $\frac{1}{8}$ in. from the lines, then a second cut $\frac{1}{32}$ in. from the line, and finally cutting, as in Fig. 109, and then planing as before.

Some important differences exist between the necessities of side and edge planing on the one hand and end-planing on the other.

First, In side and edge planing a shaving is usually taken along the entire length of the board, as previously stated. In end-planing this must not be done, since the wood will be splintered when the plane passes off, as at A, Fig. 111. To avoid this, plane a few times from *a*, about two-thirds of the way across the end to *b*, and then a few times from *c* to *d*, thus alternating till the end is complete.

Second, When planing sides or edges, be careful to hold the plane parallel to the direction of the shaving, as in Fig. 103. When planing ends, it is better to hold the block-plane at an angle to the direction of the shaving, as in Fig. 108, more clearly illustrated in the diagram, Fig. 112, which shows a block-plane commencing and finishing a stroke.

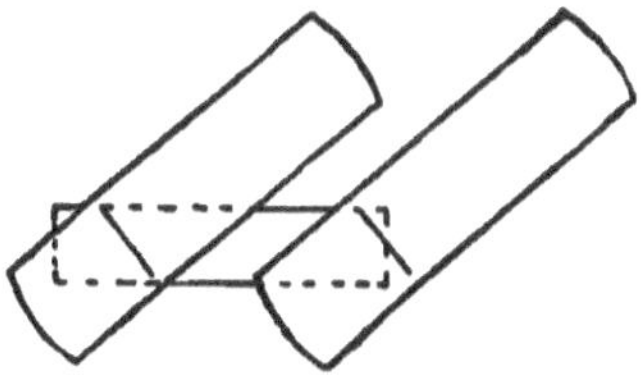

Fig. 112.

Measure 8 in. from the finished end, square around, saw (chisel if necessary), and plane to lines as before.

Treat all four boards in like manner; though, as stated before, rapid workmen will complete all four, and perhaps more, while slower workmen are making but one or two.

Mark according to power finally acquired in accurate planing.

Problem III. To make a Bread-Board.—For practice in truing wider surfaces than the preceding, take a white wood board $\frac{7}{8}$ in. thick, roughly sawed, $12\frac{1}{2}$ in. × $9\frac{1}{2}$ in., true both sides, as in Lesson VII., and both edges and ends as in the present lesson, making it 12 in. × 9 in. On one side of the board measure from each corner 3 in. along each edge and 2 in. along each end, and draw pencil-lines, as in Fig. 113.

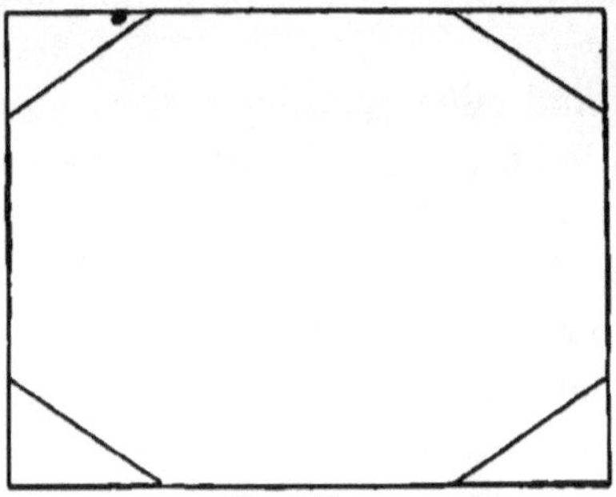

Fig. 113.

Square across edges and ends, and make corresponding lines on the opposite side. Saw near to and plane exactly to these

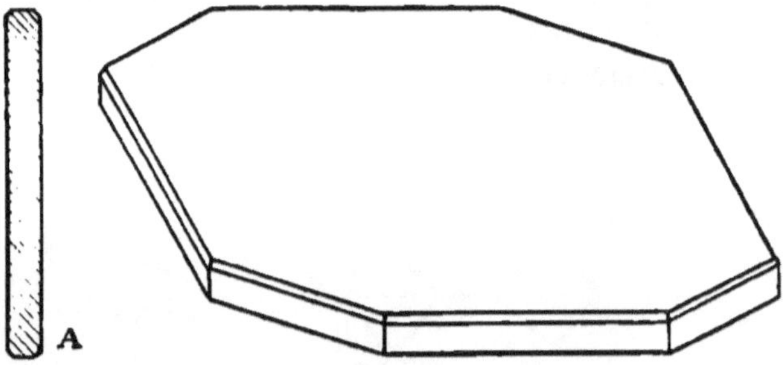

Fig. 114.

lines, thus observing all four of the fundamental rules. Chamfer the corners as follows: Hold the work in the vise, and with fine-set plane take off the corners, making instead new faces

$\frac{1}{8}$ in. wide at an angle of 45 degrees with the sides of the board, giving the finished work the appearance of Fig. 114. The larger view in this figure is a perspective, and allows only four of the chamfered corners to show. The smaller view at A is a section.

Take a quarter of a sheet of No. $\frac{1}{2}$ sand-paper, fold it over a block, and sand-paper the completed work, without marring any corners. This board is a useful article in the home to lay a loaf of bread on while cutting it.

LESSON IX.

USE OF BIT AND BRAD-AWL.

Problem I. Boring across the Grain. — Take one of the boards 8 in. × $2\frac{3}{4}$ in. × $\frac{7}{8}$ in. planed in the last two lessons, and set the gauge to one-half its thickness, thus: —

Measure the thickness of the board, set the gauge one-half of the amount, and on one edge of the board gauge a point from each side, as in Fig. 115.

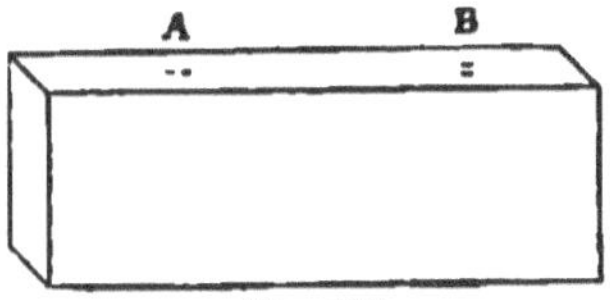

Fig. 115.

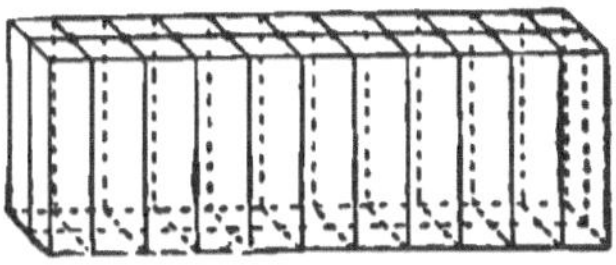

Fig. 116.

If these points coincide, as at A, the gauge is correctly adjusted. If they do not coincide, as at B, change the gauge slightly and gauge two more points, thus trying till they do coincide.

Gauge from the tried face (See Fig. 105, Lesson VIII.) on both edges of the board, and with the knife square around at $\frac{5}{8}$ in. from one end and afterwards at every $\frac{3}{4}$ in., as in Fig. 116.

Place the board in the vise with an edge uppermost, taking care that it is secured in a horizontal position. With one leg of the dividers held vertically, press a point at each intersection of lines deep enough to hold the spur of the bit.

Fasten the $\frac{1}{4}$ in. auger bit in the bit-brace, place its spur in one of these points, stand in front of the bench, and holding the brace as in Fig. 117, turn it two or three revolutions, watching to see that it stands vertical as viewed from that position.

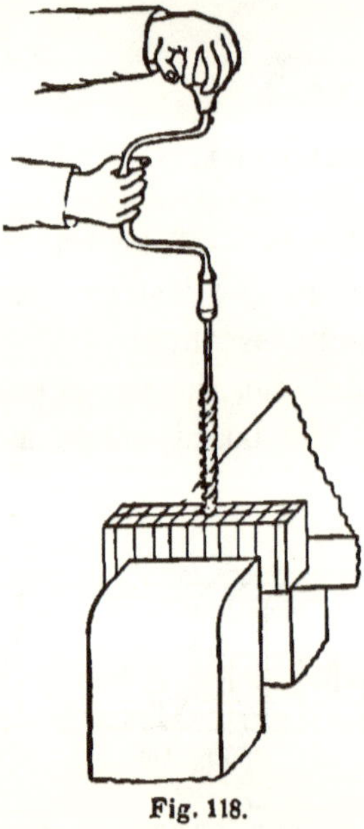

Fig. 118.

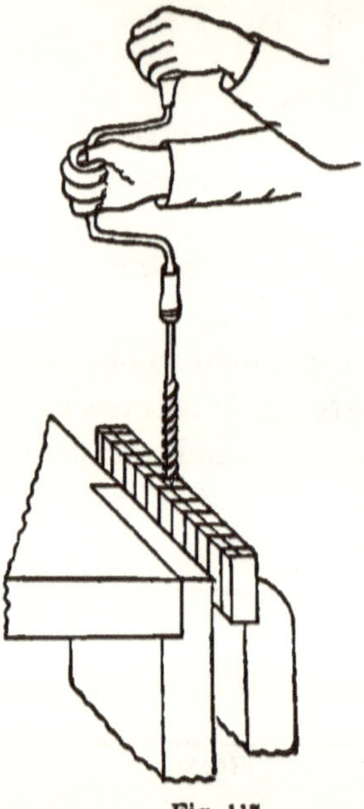

Fig. 117.

Cease boring, move to a position at the end of the bench, as in Fig. 118, and observing the above directions turn the brace two or three more revolutions. Resume the first position and repeat. Alternate thus between these two positions, revolving the brace two or three times in each, taking great care that the bit stands vertical as viewed from either position, and that it is never pushed from or toward you, thereby disturbing the vertical adjustment of the previous position. The first inch of depth in boring will give direction to the hole. It cannot be changed much after that.

When the bit is nearly through the board, place the finger underneath at every revolution of the brace, and when the spur is felt, cease boring. Now turn the brace backward *two* revolutions to loosen the spur, and then draw it out, either without revolving it at all, or revolving it *forward.* This is to clean the boring-chips out of the hole, for if the bit is revolved backward while it is being withdrawn the boring chips will remain in the hole. Note this and remember it.

Bore at every intersection of lines in like manner. The under side of the work will present a succession of points nearly or quite agreeing with the intersection of lines thereon.

Mark 10 off from 100 for every point that varies $\frac{1}{8}$ in. from the intersection which it should meet.

It will be noticed that we have used the smallest auger bit, though a larger one is represented in Figs. 117 and 118, for clearness of illustration. We use the $\frac{1}{4}$ in. because all the principles involved can be taught with it as well as with any size, because greater care is necessary with it than with a larger one, and because it is found that notwithstanding its frailty the percentage of breakage is too small to need taking into account.

Problem. II. Boring with the Grain.—Take another of the boards planed in the last two lessons, cut it $5\frac{1}{2}$ in. long, gauge midway of the thickness on each edge and end, and gauge at successive $1\frac{1}{6}$ in. from the tried edge (See Fig. 105, Lesson VIII. for definition of tried edge), on each side and end, as in Fig. 119.

Place the work in the vise with an end uppermost. It should stand exactly vertical, with one-half of it buried in the vise. Bore as directed in Figs. 117 and 118 till one-half of the spiral portion of the bit is buried in the wood, as in Fig. 120, when the bit should be withdrawn to clean out the boring-chips from the hole. Use the same precaution in withdrawing as directed in Problem I.

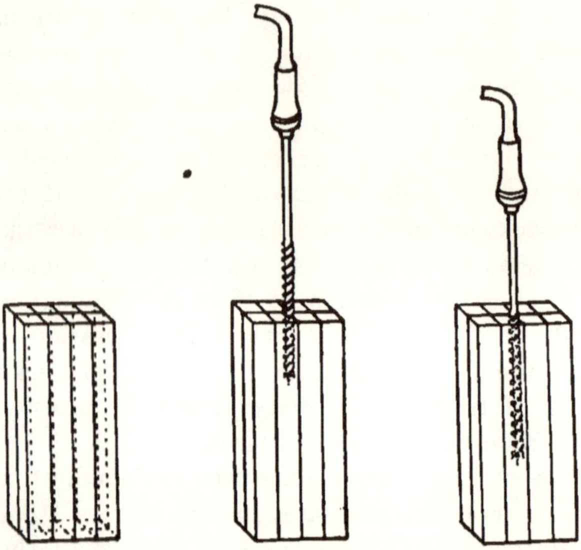

Fig. 119. Fig. 120. Fig. 121.

Insert the bit in the hole, and bore till the spiral is all buried, as in Fig. 121, then withdraw as before.

Insert the bit in the hole, and bore an inch deeper and withdraw, and so continue till the bit comes through at the lower end.

These directions concerning cleaning out chips *must* be observed or the bit will be either broken or bent. If they are observed, it need never be injured.

Mark 10 off from 100 for every hole that comes out $\frac{1}{4}$ in. from its proper intersection.

Problem. III. Boring from both Ends.—Take one of the boards planed in last lesson, gauge it as in Problem II., and bore it as in that problem about 5 in. deep. Invert it in the vise, and bore from the other end till the holes meet midway.

Mark 10 off from 100 for every hole which you cannot see through.

Problem IV. Use of Drill-Bit. — Take one of the boards planed in the last two lessons, make it 2 in. wide, gauge and square as in Problem I., and bore holes as in that problem, using the $\frac{5}{32}$ in. drill-bit. At first this bit will need no downward pressure beyond the weight of the bit-stock; but when the point of the bit has descended half an inch in the wood it will be necessary to hold back on it, or it will descend faster than it can cut, and the result will be a small rough hole, and perhaps a broken bit. Note this also and remember it.

Problem V. Use of Brad-Awl. — Take another of the boards planed in the last two lessons or a similar one; gauge on both sides at every $\frac{11}{16}$ in., and square around at $\frac{5}{8}$ in. from one end, and then at every $\frac{3}{4}$ in., as in Fig. 122.

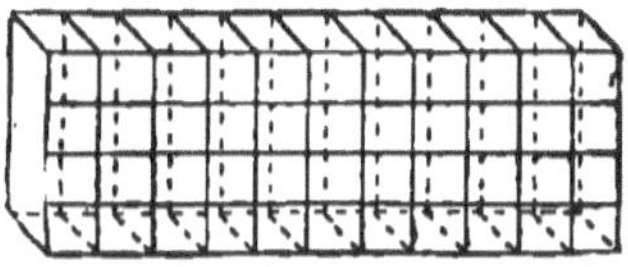

Fig. 122.

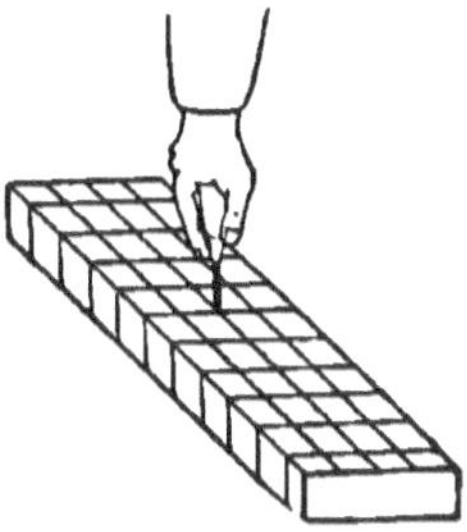

Fig. 123.

With medium-sized awl bore from the intersection of lines on one side of the board a little more than half way through, as in Fig. 123, then turn the board over and bore from the intersection on the other side to meet the first bored holes, sighting from two directions at right angles to each other, as in boring with the auger bit, in order to insure a vertical hole.

Mark 2 off from 100 for every hole which you cannot see through.

LESSON X.

SHOVE-PLANING.

Wood as thin as $\frac{1}{4}$ in. cannot be easily planed square on edges and ends by holding it in the vise, and resort is had to a contrivance known as the shove-plane, or shoot-plane board (Fig. 124), which may be bolted to the front right end of the bench by two carriage-bolts, one of which is shown in front section in Fig. 125. This arrangement provides for its being quickly put in position or removed.

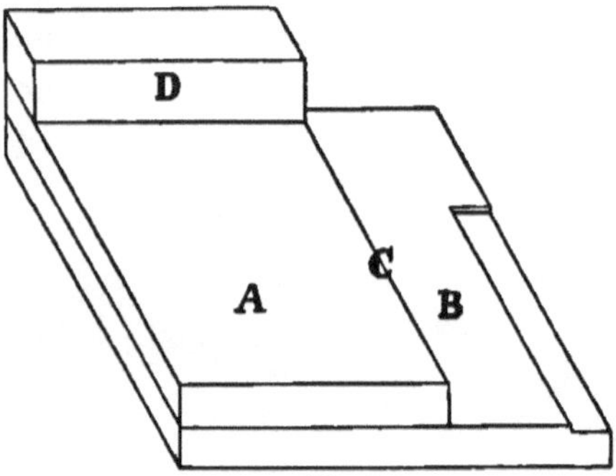

Fig. 124.

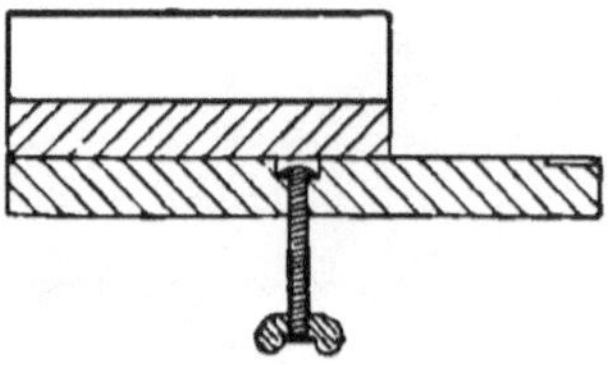

Fig. 125.

The surfaces A and B are made parallel to each other, and the edges C and D are perpendicular to them.

Problem I. Finishing to a Width. — Provide for each pupil a $\frac{1}{4}$ in. pine board about 5 ft. long by 5 in. wide. Saw from it roughly a piece $4\frac{1}{2}$ in. long. Be sure that the plane-blade is finely set, as directed in Lesson VII. Lay the work on the surface A, with its end resting against D, its edge overhanging C about $\frac{1}{4}$ in. and hold it in that position firmly with the left hand as in Fig. 126. Lay the finishing-plane on its right side on the surface B, and holding it firmly in contact with that surface, make with it the least number of strokes necessary to true the edges of the work, as in Fig. 126.

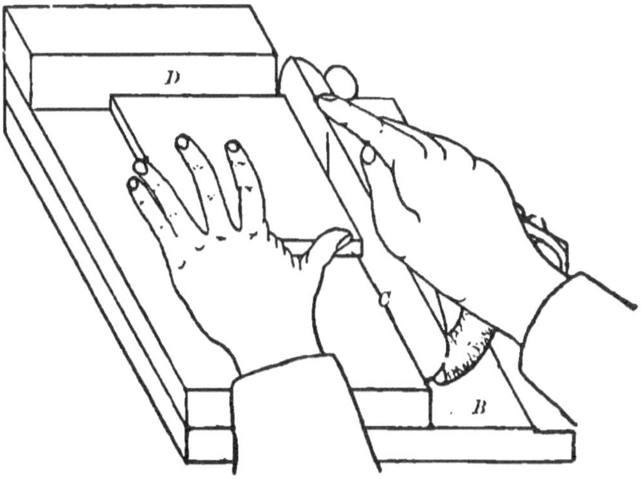

Fig. 126.

With the help of the rule set the gauge $\frac{3}{4}$ in. *plus*, as in Fig. 127.

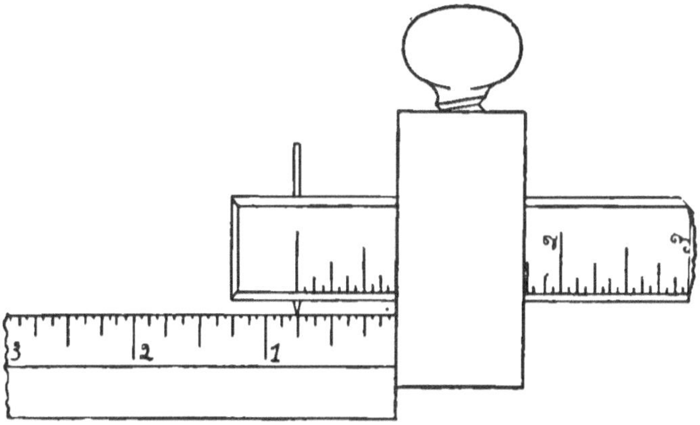

Fig. 127.

The help of the rule is required since the gauge-point is not always accurately against the zero graduation of the gauge.

By the term *plus* is meant a small fraction over ¾ in., as is seen in Fig. 127, where the gauge-point does not meet the centre of the ¾ in. graduation, but meets that side of it which is farthest from zero.

With the gauge set as directed, gauge from the finished edge on both sides of the work, draw the knife-blade a few times in the gauge-line, as in Fig. 128, on both sides, and the wood will split apart.

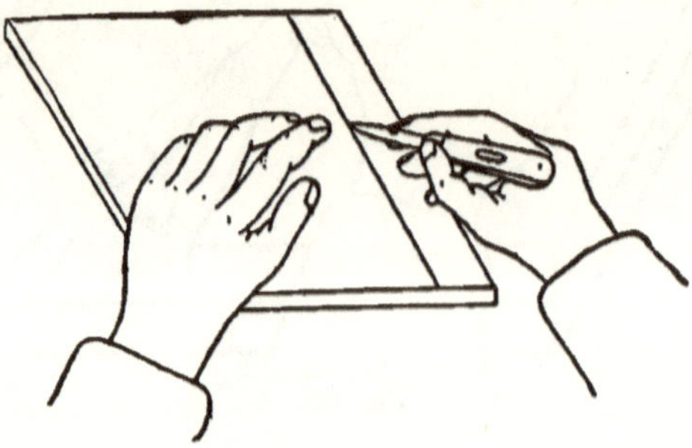

Fig. 128.

Shove-plane the split edge of the ¾ piece just enough to true it, and leave it ¾ in. Again we must press the importance of having the plane set fine. Let accurate workmen make as many pieces ¾ in. wide as they have time, while slower workmen are mastering the difficulties of making one or two.

Problem II. Finishing to a Length. — Take one of the pieces planed to a width in Problem I., hold it as in Fig. 129, and plane an end, using the block-plane finely set.

In this operation the face of the block-plane needs to be held against the shoulder C, and a little more force is used with the right hand to keep the plane in contact with C than is used with the left hand to keep the work in contact with the plane.

It will be found helpful to divide every shove of the plane into four actions, thus: —

First, Hold the plane very firmly against C and B, with its edge in front of the work.

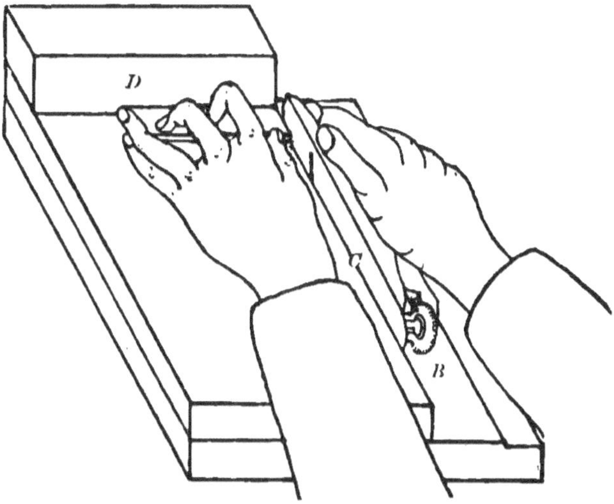

Fig. 129.

Second, Slide the work firmly against the plane, keeping it in contact with D.

Third, Shove the plane forward, keeping both it and the work in place.

Fourth, Relax the muscles of both hands, and bring the plane back, ready to repeat the first action.

A few shoves of the plane should finish one end of the work, and, if the shove-plane block is in order, the work will be true. The plane, however, *must* be kept finely set, or the accuracy of the shove-plane board will be destroyed.

From the finished end of the work measure 2 in. *plus*, square around using knife and try-square, saw near to lines using 10 in. back-saw, and saw block similar to Fig. 107, Lesson VIII., and shove plain exactly to line.

Finish several boards thus to a length, and lay their sides together, as in Fig. 130. If the work has all been accurate, they will agree with each other in lengths and widths.

Lay their edges together, as in Fig. 131, and four of them will cover 3 in. width. Lay their ends together, as in Fig.

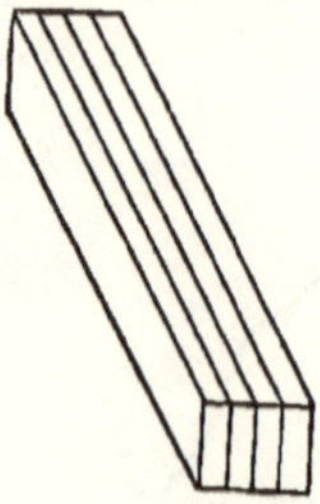

Fig. 130.

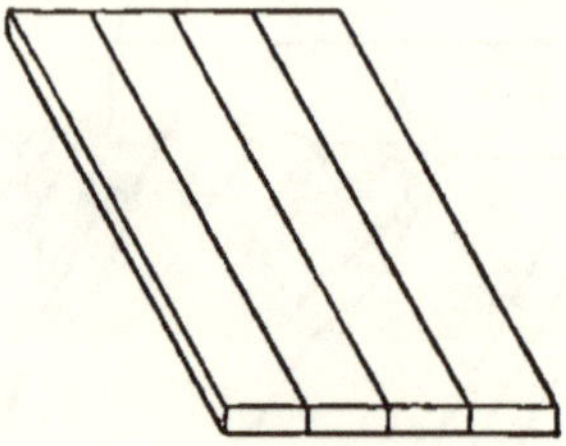

Fig. 131.

132, and three of them will make a length of 6 in., or six of 12 in.

Fig 132

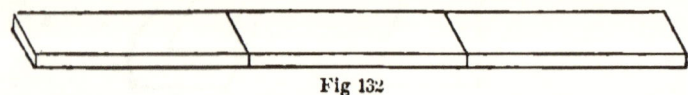

Problem III. To make from ¼ in. Stock a Box 4 in. × 2 in.

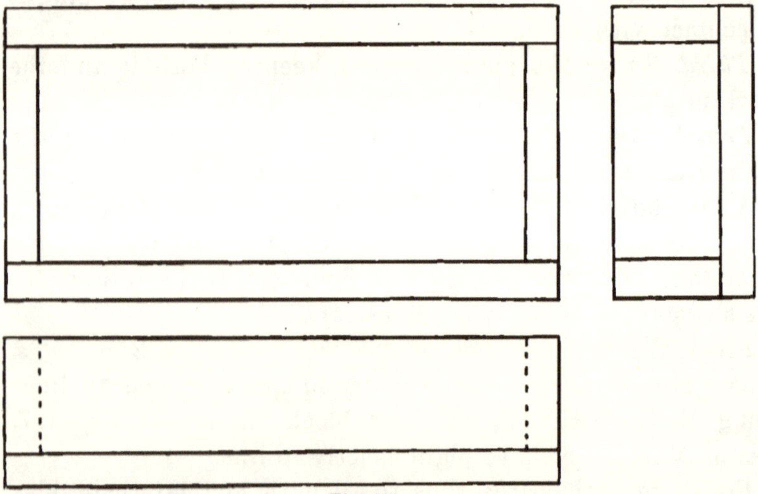

Fig. 133.

× 1 *in. Outside Measure.* — Make a full-sized drawing, showing three views of the box, top, side, and end, as in Fig. 133.

From a study of these drawings obtain the dimensions of the bottom board, and also the sides and ends. Set the figures down in some convenient place. According to the figures make one bottom board, two sides and two ends. Use $\frac{5}{8}$ in. No. 20 steel wire brads, and nail first the sides and ends together to form a frame, putting two nails in each end of a side piece spaced as in Fig. 134.

Fig. 134.

Nail the bottom to the frame, spacing the nails as in Fig. 135. Before nailing the sides and ends, however, hold them together and see if they make a width just equal to the bottom.

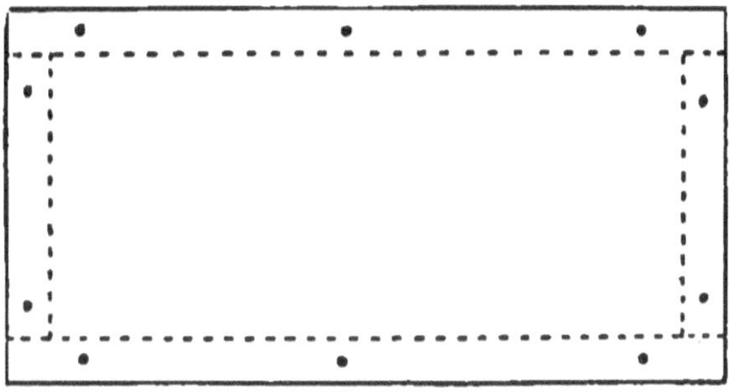

Fig. 135.

Let accurate rapid workmen make a box 5 in. × $2\frac{1}{2}$ in. × $1\frac{1}{4}$ in.

Problem IV. Fig. 136 is a full-size end view of a box whose frame has the same dimensions as Problem III., and which has a chamfered bottom of $\frac{1}{4}$ in. stock, and a chamfered and rabbited cover of $\frac{3}{8}$ in. stock. Lay out the chamfer lines on the edges and ends of boards with the gauge. Lay out the chamfer lines on the sides of boards with pencil, or if gauge is used make very light lines. Lay out lines for rabbit with gauge where they run lengthwise of the grain, and with try-square and knife where they run crosswise; plane the chamfers. Cut the rabbit with the knife.

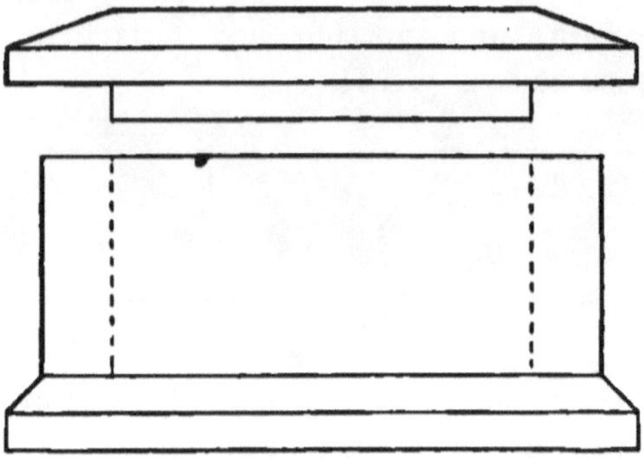

Fig. 136.

Two partitions fitted as in the half-size views, Fig. 137, will divide the box in three compartments convenient for holding postage-stamps.

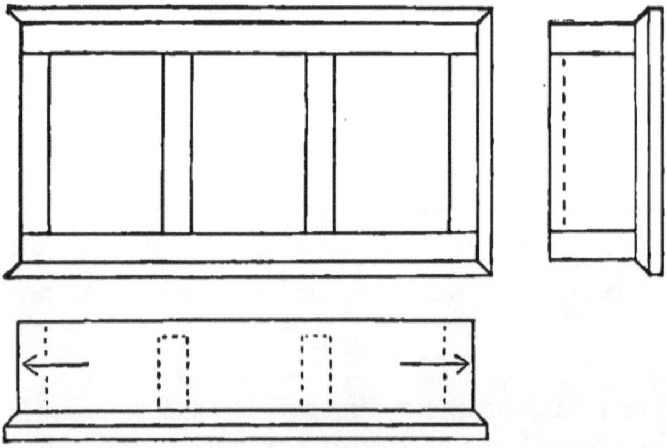

Fig. 137

LESSON XI.

SQUARE, PRISM, AND CYLINDER.

Problem I. Square Prism 8 *in.* × $1\frac{3}{4}$ *in.* × $1\frac{3}{4}$ *in.*—Supply each pupil with a piece of $1\frac{7}{8}$ in. planed pine plank $8\frac{1}{2}$ in. long × any width. Draw pencil-lines lengthwise on one side of it 2 in. apart. Square lines across each end, and join them by lines on the back side, as in Fig. 138.

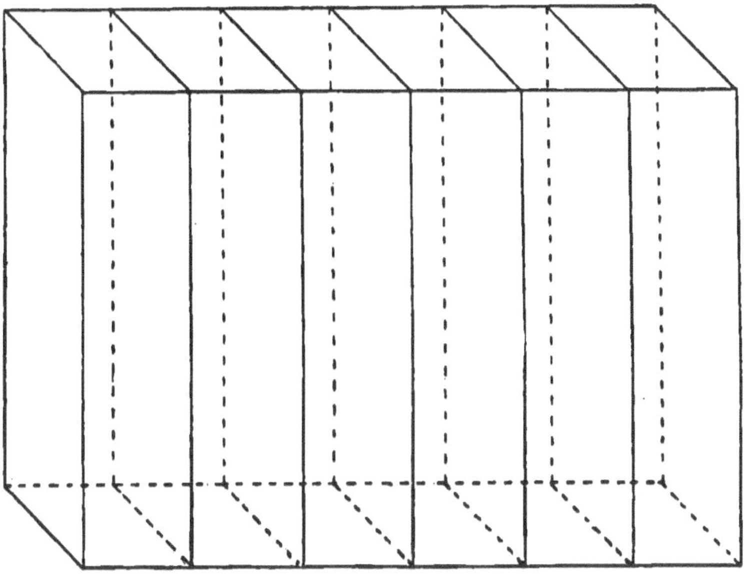

Fig. 138.

Place the work in the vise, and saw *on* these lines. See that the saw keeps on the lines on the back side of the work as well as on the front side. If difficulty is experienced, it may be wise to occasionally turn the work about in the vise, so as to bring that which is the back side to the front. Saw at least two pieces. Rapid workmen, if accurate, may saw five or six.

Rough-plane the two sawed sides of each piece sufficiently to remove saw-marks, observing carefully all directions given in Lesson VII.

Finish-plane one side of a piece as directed in connection with Figs. 97–100, Lesson VII., and write your name on it, as in Fig. 139.

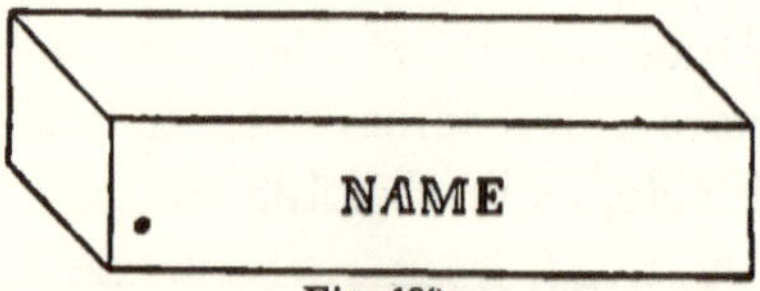

Fig. 139.

Plane an adjacent side, following directions given in Problem I., Lesson VIII., except imagining a division in three sections instead of two. When this second side is complete, place tried marks on it, as in Fig. 140.

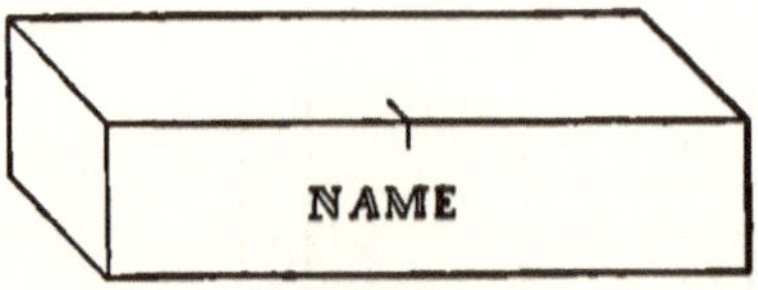

Fig. 140.

Set the gauge 1¾ in. *plus,* and gauge from the first finished side on both of the sides adjacent to it, as in Fig. 141.

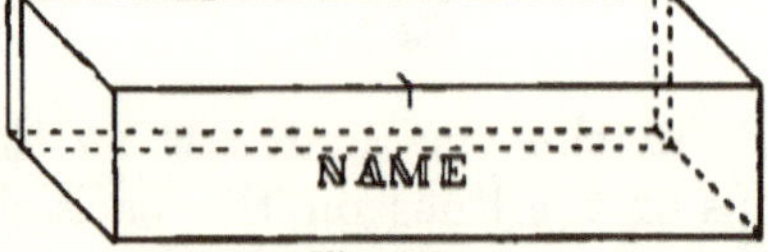

Fig. 141.

Rough-plane nearly to these lines, if necessary, *Rule III.*, and finish-plane exactly to them. *Rule IV.*, when a third side of the prism is completed.

With the same setting of the gauge, gauge from the second finished side, and complete the fourth side of the prism in like manner. Use try-square and knife, and square around about ¼ in. from one end, as in Fig. 142.

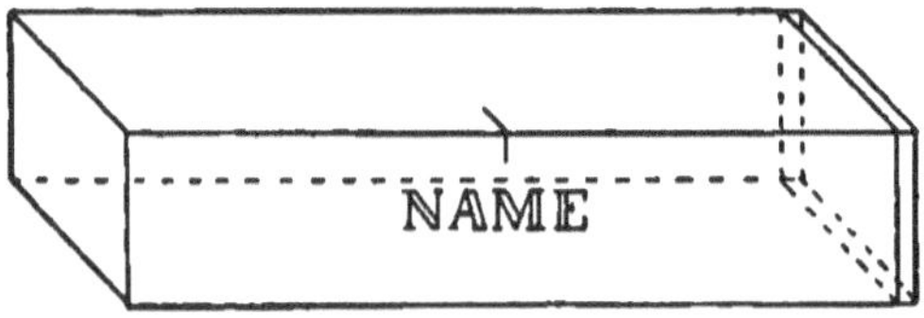

Fig. 142.

Hold the work on the saw-block, as in Fig. 107, Lesson VIII., and saw about one-third of the way through. Turn it one-quarter of a revolution from you, and saw likewise. Turn it another quarter and repeat, and still another quarter and saw completely off. By thus turning and partial sawing, one can saw closer to the line than otherwise.

Hold the work in the vise, and plane, as in Fig. 108, Lesson VIII. Plane from all four sides and corners to and a little past the centre, observing Rule IV.

From the end so finished measure 8 in. *plus*, and finish the other end. Make three such prisms 8 in. × 1¾ in. × 1¾ in.

Problem II. Octagonal Prism. — Describe on drawing-paper a circle 1¾ in. diameter, and draw a square around it, as in Fig. 143.

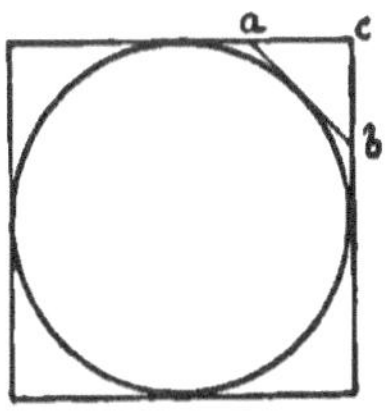

Fig. 143.

Draw also the line *a b* at the angle of 45°. The distance *a c* measures ½ in. *plus*. Set the gauge ½ in., and gauge two

lines on each of the four sides of one of the prisms, as in Fig. 144.

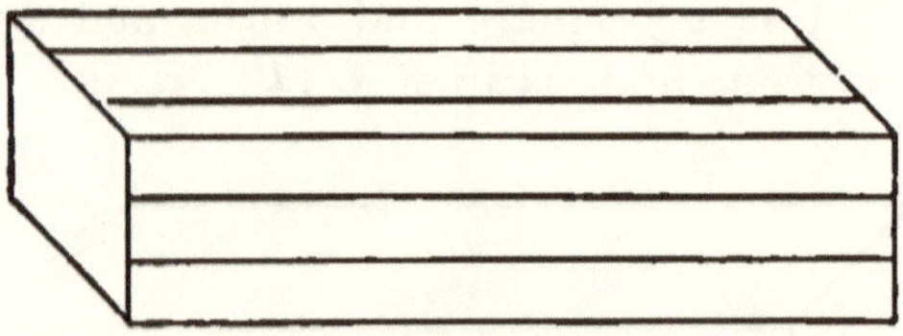

Fig. 144.

Hold the work in the vise, and plane to these lines, as in Fig. 145, when you have an octagonal prism.

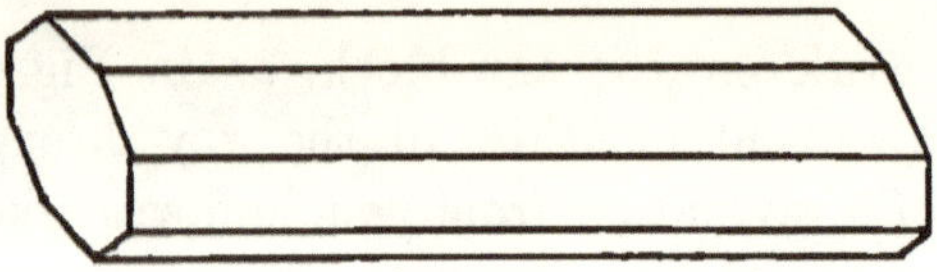

Fig. 145.

Problem III. Cylinder. — Make a second octagonal prism, and exercise skill to so plane away its corners as to make a 16-sided prism. Again plane away these corners so as to make a 32-sided prism, then a 64-sided prism, and sand-paper it to a cylinder.

For another method centre each end of a $1\frac{3}{4}$ in. square prism, describe $1\frac{3}{4}$ in. circles thereon, and plane the corners away till these circles are reached.

LESSON XII.

USE OF CHISEL AND GOUGE.

Some instructions were given in Lesson VIII. concerning handling the chisel which are not necessary to repeat here.

Problem I. Locked Joint. — Make, as in Lessons VII. and VIII., two boards $4\frac{1}{2}$ in. × 2 in. × $\frac{7}{8}$ in.

Gauge from one edge of each on both of its sides $\frac{3}{4}$ in. Place points on the edge at every $\frac{3}{4}$ in., and through them, square lines across the edge; also continue the lines, squaring on each side as far as to the gauged line, when the work will appear as in Fig. 146.

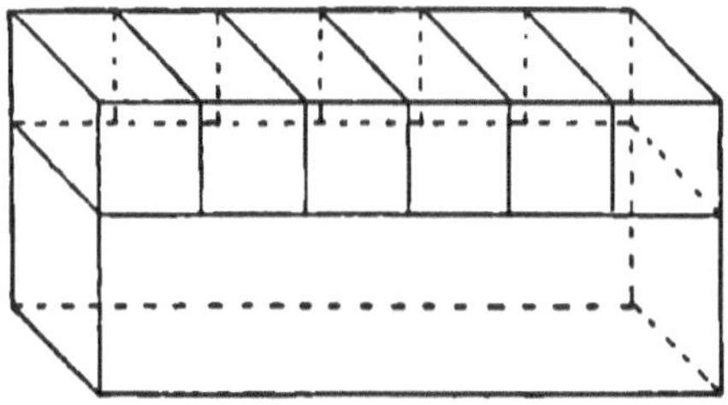

Fig. 146.

Remove each alternate section by sawing near to lines and then chiselling exactly to them, as in Fig. 147.

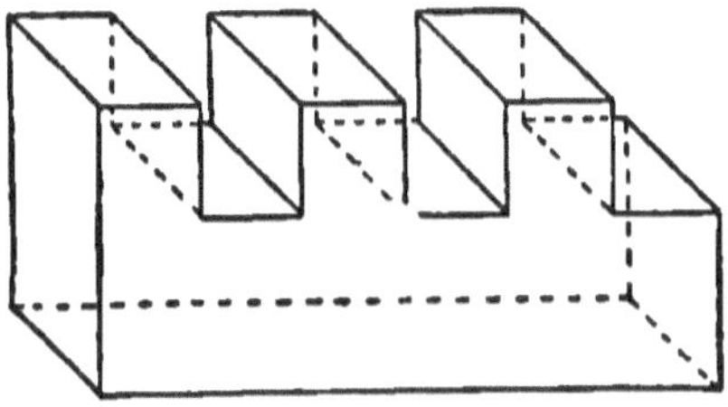

Fig. 147.

When accurately made, the two boards will fit together, as in Fig. 148.

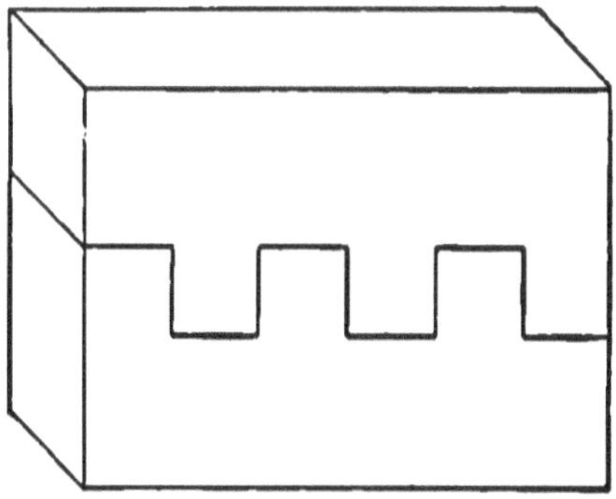

Fig. 148.

Problem II. Chiselled Pyramids.—Make a board 5 in. × 3 in. × 7/8 in. On one side of it draw lines lengthwise at every ½ in., using rule and pencil, and crosswise at every ½ in., using try-square and pencil.

From that side gauge ½ in. on each edge and end, and square down to these last lines from the lines on the top, when the work will appear as in Fig. 149.

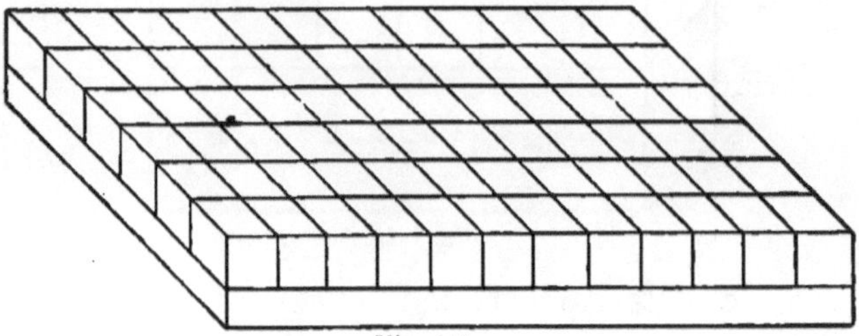

Fig. 149.

Make saw-kerfs on alternate crosswise lines, as in Fig. 150. Draw necessary bevelled lines on each end at an angle of

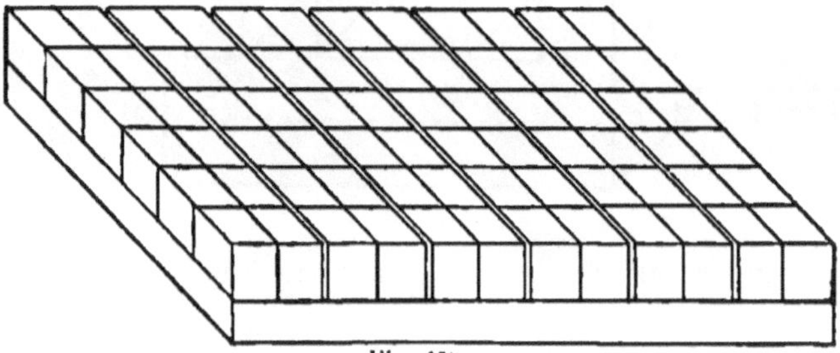

Fig. 150.

45°, and chisel lengthwise to them, giving the work the appearance of Fig. 151.

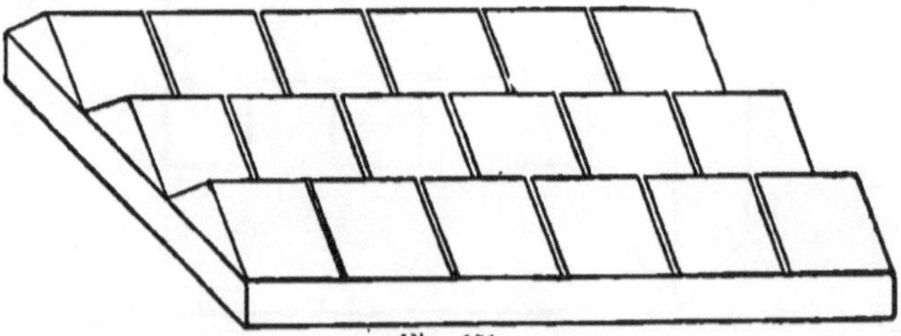

Fig. 151.

With rule and pencil restore the points that are to be apices of pyramids. Make a cardboard templet to the angle which the base of a pyramid is to make with an edge; use it to draw necessary pencil lines, and chisel V grooves crosswise of the board, leaving rows of square pyramids, as in Fig. 152.

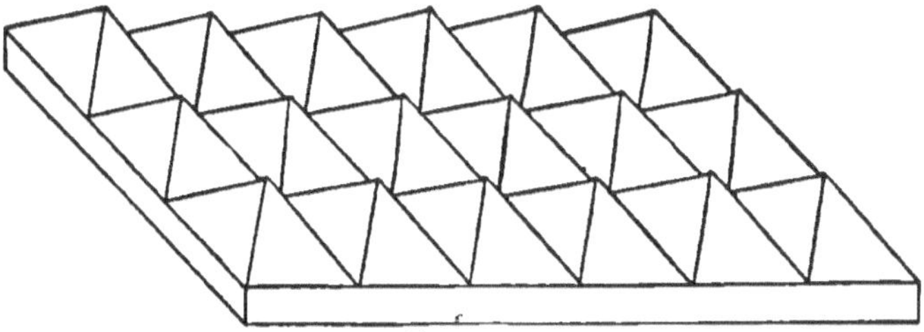

Fig 152.

Problem III. Chamfered Corners.—Make a square prism 8 in. × $1\frac{3}{4}$ in. × $1\frac{3}{4}$ in. Rapid workmen may plane the ends. Square around fine pencil lines 1 in. and $1\frac{3}{8}$ in. from each end. Set the gauge $\frac{3}{8}$ in., and gauge two lines on every side between the two $1\frac{3}{8}$ in. squared lines, as in Fig. 153. Join the points *a* and *b*.

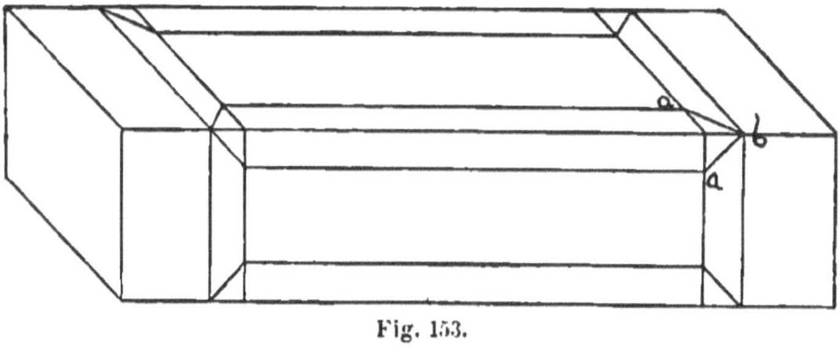

Fig. 153.

Put a thin keen edge on the 1 in. chisel, and cut to these lines, as in Fig. 154.

A corner cut away in this manner is called a chamfer. Pupils who work slowly need not plane this block on the end.

Problem IV. Use of Outside Ground Gouge. — Repeat the

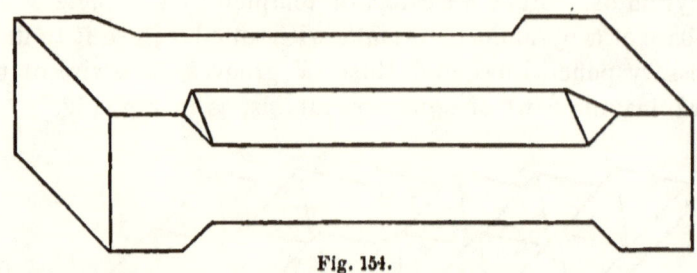

Fig. 154.

last problem, using $\frac{3}{4}$ in. outside ground-gouge, and give the finished work the appearance of Fig. 155.

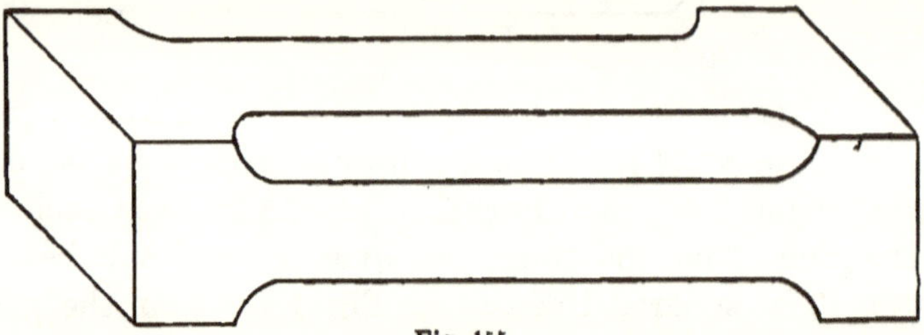

Fig. 155.

Problem V. Use of Inside Ground-Gouge across the Grain. — Make a board $5\frac{5}{8}$ in. × $3\frac{1}{8}$ in. × $\frac{7}{8}$ in. On one side of it square knife-lines across at every $\frac{5}{8}$ in., and cut out each

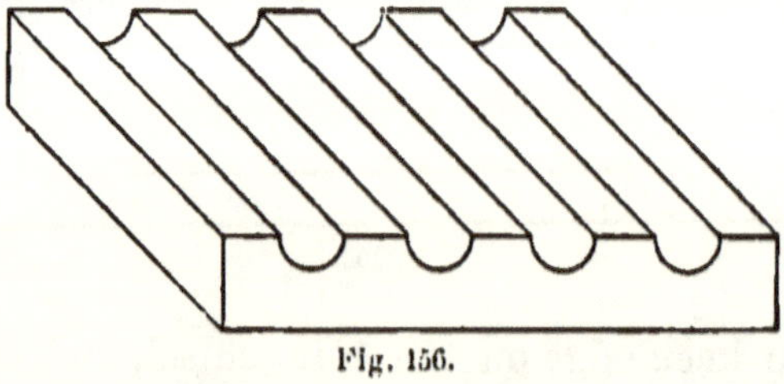

Fig. 156.

alternate section with the $\frac{1}{2}$ in. inside ground-gouge, making semi-cylindrical grooves, as in Fig. 156.

Test the accuracy of the work by using a right-triangle.

The corner of the try-square blade will answer, as in Fig. 157. The value of this test depends on the fact that every angle inscribed in a semi-circle is a right-angle.

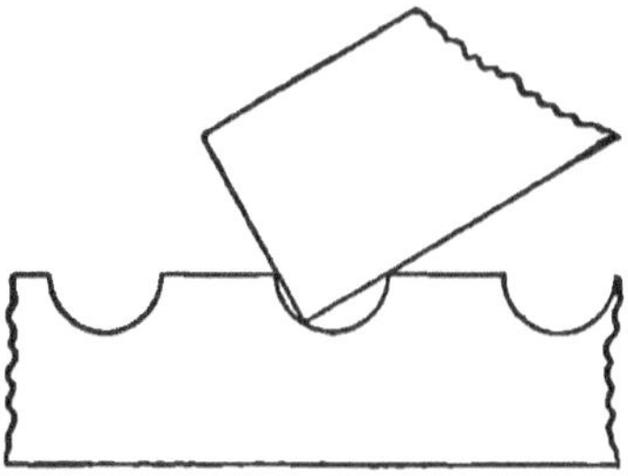

Fig. 157.

Problem VI. Use of the Inside Gouge Lengthwise of the Grain. — On the opposite side of the board used in Problem V., gauge lines at every $\frac{5}{8}$ in., and, operating in a manner

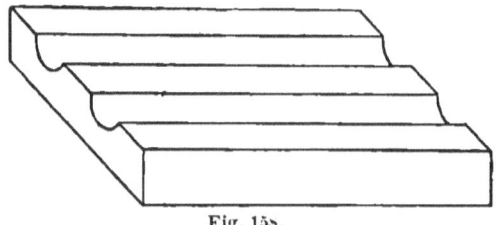

Fig. 158.

similar to Problem V., make semi-cylindrical grooves in alternate sections, as in Fig. 158.

LESSON XIII.

HAND-SCREW AND SCREW-DRIVER.

Problem I. Adjusting the Hand-Screw. — The use of the hand-screw is to hold work in place on the bench, or to hold two pieces firmly together while glue is drying. It is necessary to keep the jaws constantly parallel, else inconvenience will result in adjusting, or injury in clamping. If through inadvertence the parallelism of the jaws is disturbed, one of the screws must be turned independently of the other, sufficient to correct it. Fig. 159 shows a hand screw correctly adjusted, that is, with its jaws parallel.

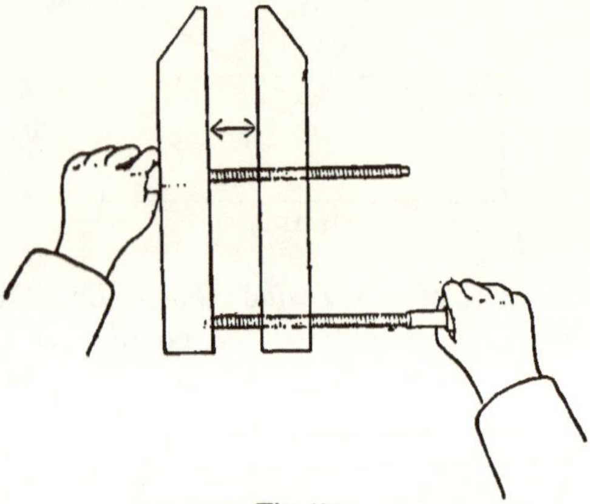

Fig. 159.

Set the hand-screw so that the distance between the jaws near the inner screw (see arrow-heads, Fig. 159) shall measure a given amount, as 2 in. Next set it to some other given amount, as 4 in. To do this, grasp the outer screw with the right hand, and the inner screw with the left. Do not let either screw slip in the hand. Revolve the hand-screw, causing the upper portion to move from you and the lower portion toward you, till you judge the jaws to be 4 in. apart, then lay the tool on the bench and measure it. If the measurement is near 4 in., make it exactly so by turning the inner screw without raising the tool from the bench, but be sure to turn the outer screw at the same time, so as to keep the jaws parallel. Next, set the hand-screw to 3 in., which will necessitate revolving in the opposite direction.

In this manner practise the class in setting the hand screw to various measurements.

Problem II. Clamping-Work. — Take two blocks 4 in. × 2 in. × $\frac{7}{8}$ in. Place them with their sides together, and set the clamps to hold them lightly, as in Fig. 160.

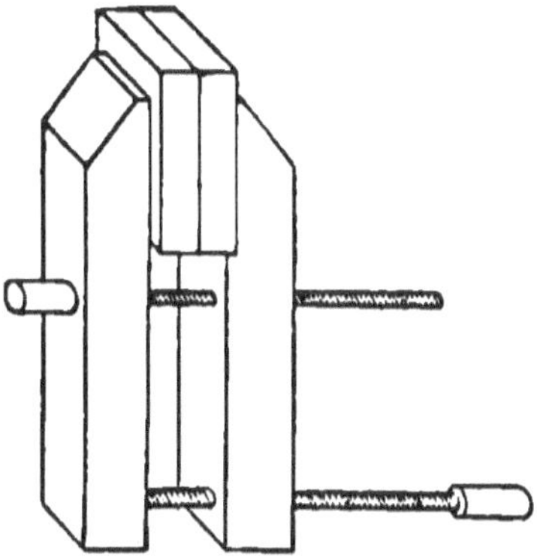

Fig. 160.

Next, tighten the grip by a hard turn of the outer screw.

Loosen the grip by first loosening the outer screw. Place the blocks with their edges together, as in Fig. 161, and clamp them in that position.

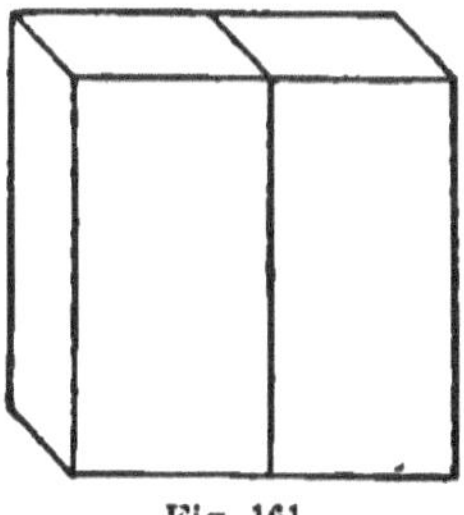

Fig. 161.

Loosen again, and place the blocks with their ends together, as in Fig. 162, and clamp them.

Place the blocks with the edge of one to a side of the other, as in Fig. 163 and clamp them.

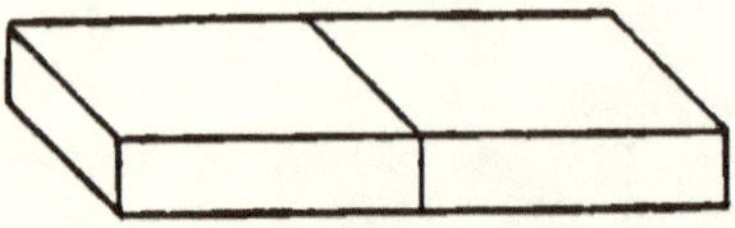

Fig. 162.

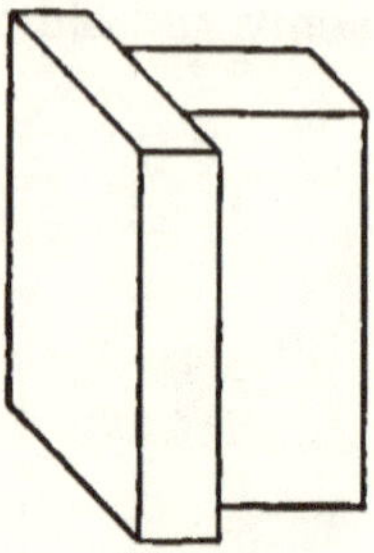

Fig. 163.

Place them with the end of one to the side of the other, as in Fig. 164 and clamp them.

Place them with the end of one to the edge of the other, as in Fig. 165 and clamp them.

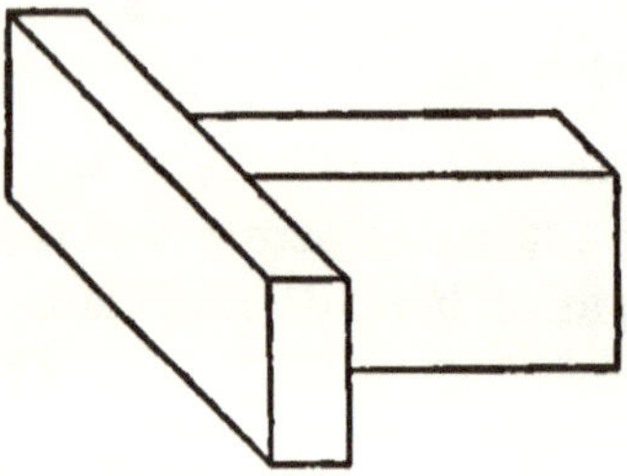

Fig. 164.

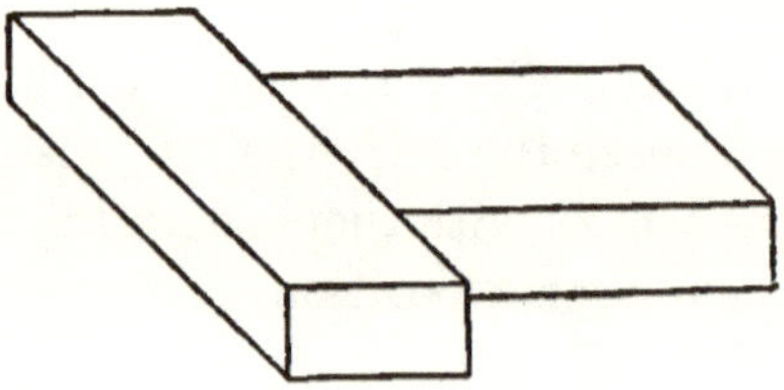

Fig. 165.

Problem III. Screw-Driving. — Take any two waste pieces of ⅞ in. pine, 8 in. × 2 in. will answer. On the piece to be

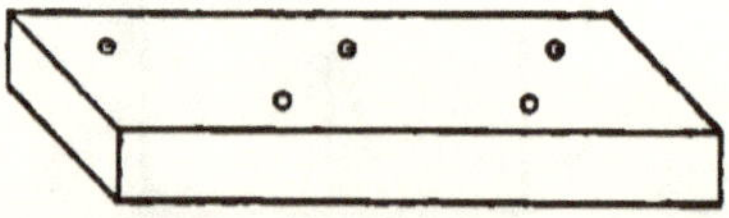

Fig. 166.

used for the upper board place several points in a zig-zag line, as in Fig. 166, about ½ in. from each edge, the points nearest the ends being about 1 in. therefrom.

Hold the board in the vise. Use the $\frac{7}{32}$ in. drill-bit, and bore holes entirely through it. No holes are needed in the under board, unless the screw is so near an end or edge as to be liable to split the wood, since screws will turn into soft pine on account of their gimlet points.

Insert a $1\frac{1}{2}$ in. No. 11 screw in each hole, and, placing the boards together, turn down each screw till its head begins to touch the wood, then press hard on the driver, turn one-half a revolution, and release. The object of this pressure is to force the screw into the wood, and the release after each semi-revolution is to prevent the driver from slipping out of the head of the screw. Keep repeating this process till the screw is forced into the wood with its top flush, or even, with the surface of the wood, as in Fig. 167. It will be noticed that we did not countersink the upper board for screw-heads, as they will force into soft pine without it.

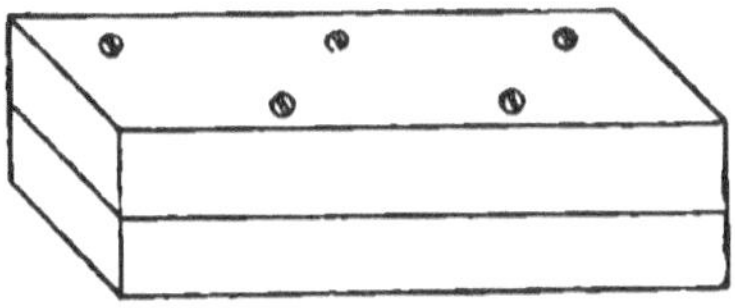

Fig. 167.

In driving No. 11 screws into hard wood it is necessary to bore with the $\frac{5}{32}$ in. drill-bit into the under piece, and to countersink the upper. It is also well to put tallow on the screw when about to turn it into hard wood.

To recapitulate: A screw requires a hole slightly larger than itself through the first board, no hole in the second, if soft wood, unless too near the end or edge, but a hole in the second board, if it be hard wood, just large enough to prevent the screw from being broken by the force required to drive it. Also the upper board if hard wood needs to be countersunk for the screw-head, while if soft wood it does not.

LESSON XIV.

TO MAKE A PAIR OF SCALES.

It is both profitable and interesting to close a series of elementary lessons by making some project or article of use. This lesson will describe one such article, and Lesson XV. another. Fig. 168 is a perspective view of a pair of scales which the average pupil can make sufficiently accurate to answer the purpose of weighing letters and papers for mail.

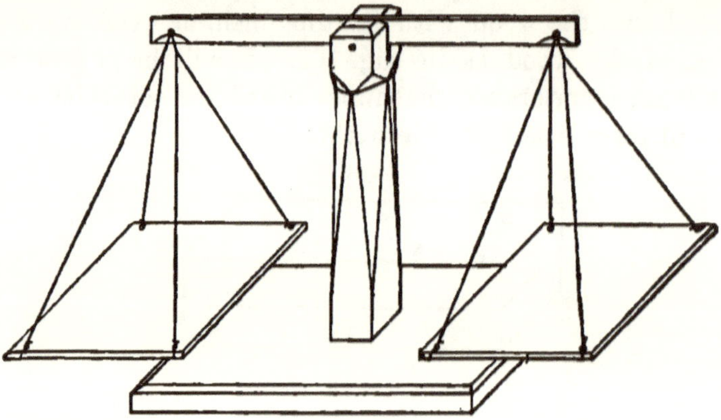

Fig. 168.

Fig. 169 shows three orthographic views of it, one-fifth size. This would make the base *a*, 8 in. × 4 in. × $\frac{1}{2}$ in.; the post *b*, 7 in. × $\frac{7}{8}$ in. × $\frac{7}{8}$ in.; the beam *c*, 10 in. × $\frac{1}{2}$ in. × $\frac{1}{8}$ in.; and the pans *d*, each 4 in. × 4 in. × $\frac{1}{8}$ in. Fig. 170 is a sectional view of a portion of the base, full size, with the post mortised into it. Fig. 171 is a quarter size elevation and plan of the post, having a tenon on the lower end, a uniform chamfer on the top, and a bevelled chamfer along most of its length, though any other design for ornamentation will answer just as well.

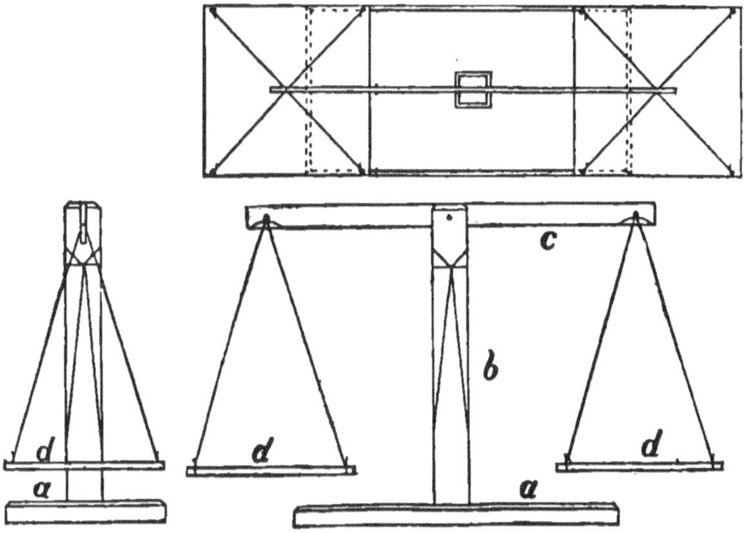

Fig. 169.

Fig. 171.

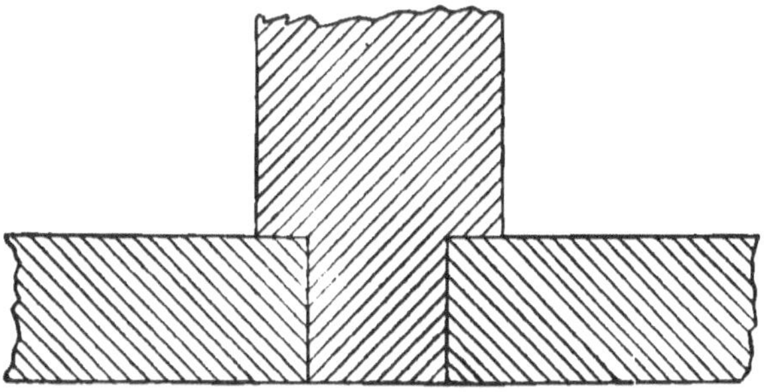

Fig. 170.

Fig. 172 is a full-size plan, front and end elevations of a portion of the beam showing places cut away on each side, to

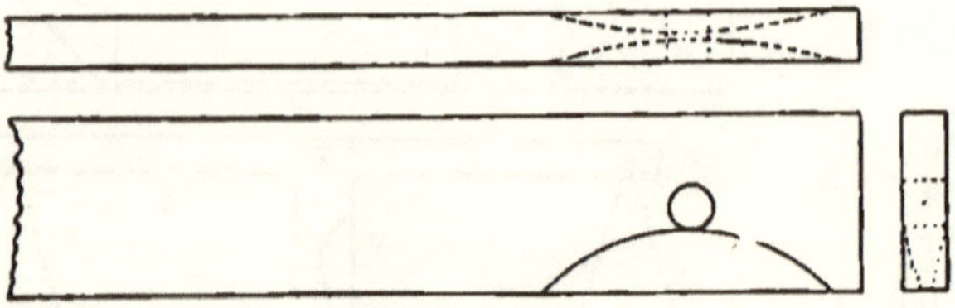

Fig. 172.

prevent friction of the cords which suspend the pans.

Fig. 173 is a full-size view of one corner of a pan, showing the hole in which the cord is tied. This hole may be ¼ in. from an end of the pan and ⅛ in. from an edge.

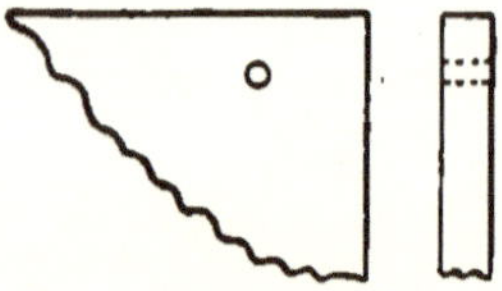

Fig. 173.

When the parts are all made and sand-papered smooth, glue the tenon of the post in the mortise of the base, and then, using a camel-hair brush about 1¼ in. wide, put a coat of thin shellac on all of the parts. Let this dry a few hours, sand-paper it sufficiently to smooth all roughness, and apply a second coat of thin shellac. Thin shellac is specified because, if it be applied too thick, a patched surface will be the result. No harm need result from too thin shellac, as, in that case, a third coat may be applied.

Shellac dries very fast, and, in applying it, take a sufficient quantity of it in the brush to cover the wood in any given place at the first stroke, and do not make a second stroke in any given place if possible. Lastly, tie on the cords and put in the nail for the beam to swing on. The hole in the beam for the nail on which it swings, and the groove in the post for the beam to play in, must both be of ample dimensions to guarantee no friction. Care is needed to tie the cords of uniform length. To facilitate this make a fixture, as in Fig. 174.

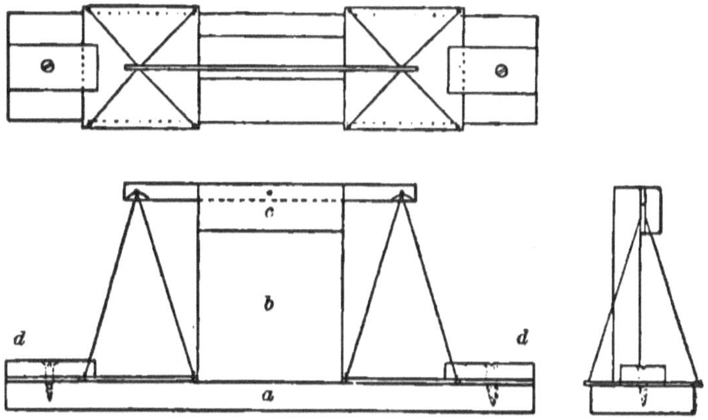

Fig. 174.

This consists of a base *a*, standard *b*, cleat *c*, and two buttons *d*, all of $\frac{7}{8}$ in. pine. By means of this fixture the beam and pans are held in proper relative position while the cords are being tied.

Fig. 175 shows an end view of the beam with a cord whose centre lies in the hole, and whose halves are then tied when the two ends can be attached to corners of a pan. Fig. 176 shows two such cords tied in one hole, leaving four projecting ends.

Care must be taken to have the holes in the ends of the beam, where the strings are tied, equidistant from the hole in the centre of the beam.

When the work is put together, if one pan proves to be heavier than the other, trim it till they are alike.

For a poise, bind four 10 *d.* wire nails in a bundle by means

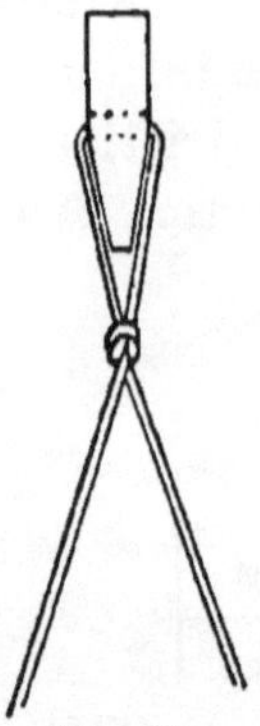

Fig. 175.

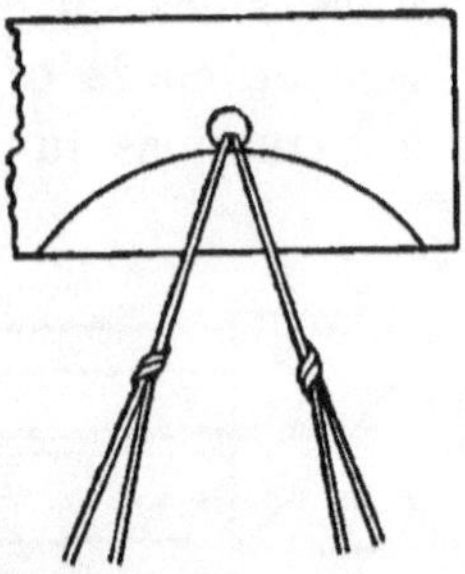

Fig. 176.

of two pieces of No. 19 soft iron wire, each $6\frac{1}{2}$ in. long, as in Fig. 177, and the whole will weigh one ounce. Place this

Fig. 177.

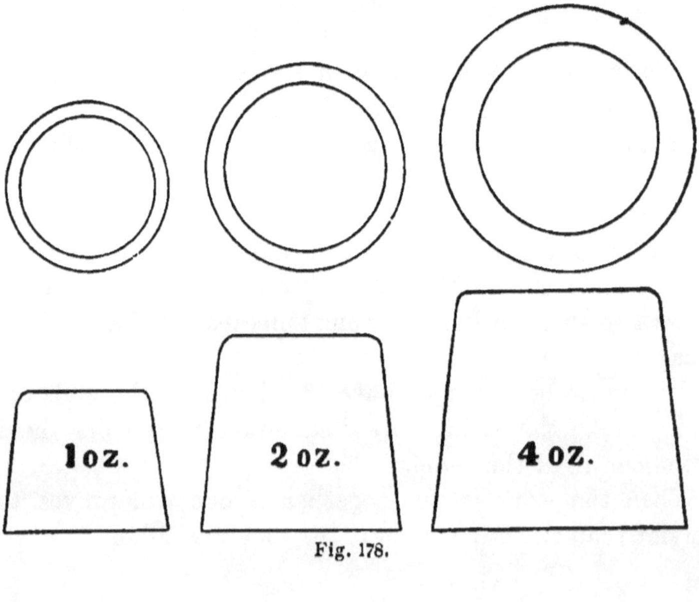

Fig. 178.

poise in one pan of the scales, and a sealed letter in the other. If the letter rises, the U. S. mail will carry it to its destination for two cents. If it balances, or falls, they will ask more.

If desired, a neat set of poises can be made of cast-iron. Fig. 178 shows three drawn full size.

These need to be cast a small fraction too heavy, and then filed to exact weight, being tested by accurate sensitive scales, each pupil filing and testing his own.

LESSON XV.

TO MAKE A BEVELLED BOX OR CARD-RECEIVER.

In this lesson, we will treat of surfaces which are bevelled with respect to each other, and for a project make a box with bevelled sides.

Problem I. The Bevelled Joint. — Fig. 179 is two views,

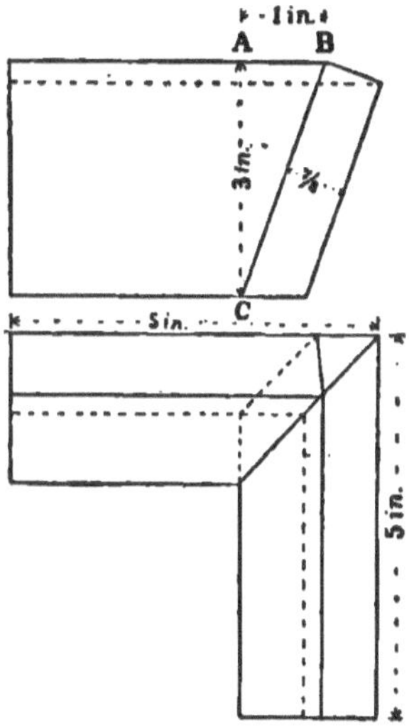

Fig. 179.

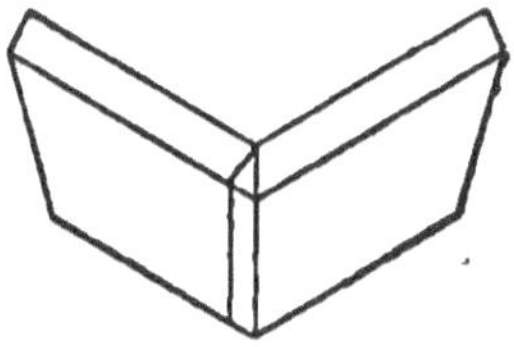
Fig. 180.

a plan and elevation of the joint to be made. Fig. 180 is a perspective view.

Draw the plan and elevation full size, and the slant height, B C will be found to be $3\frac{3}{16}$ in.

According to instructions given in Lessons VII. and VIII., finish a board 10 in. × $3\frac{3}{16}$ in. × $\frac{7}{8}$ in.

On a waste board having a true edge, E B, Fig. 181, draw the line A D square with the edge, make the distances A C = 3 in., A B = 1 in., and draw the line B C, which will = $3\frac{3}{16}$ in.

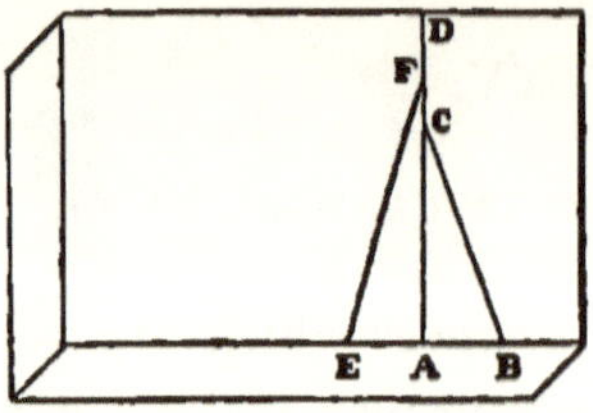

Fig. 181.

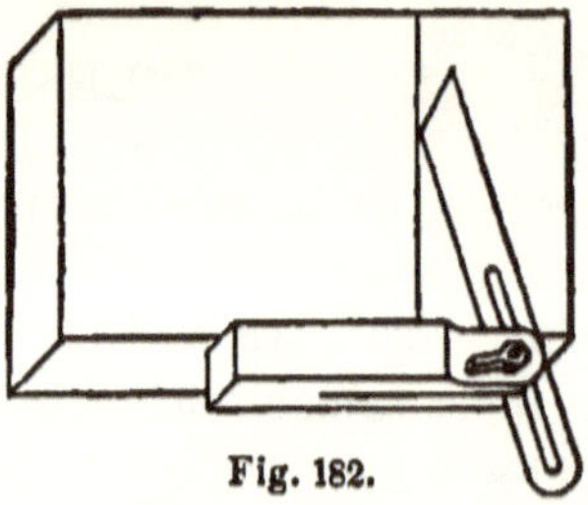

Fig. 182.

Set the bevel to this line, as in Fig. 182, and plane one edge of the 10 in. × $3\frac{3}{16}$ in. board to fit the bevel so set. The work will appear as in the outlines of Fig. 183, which shows two views of it.

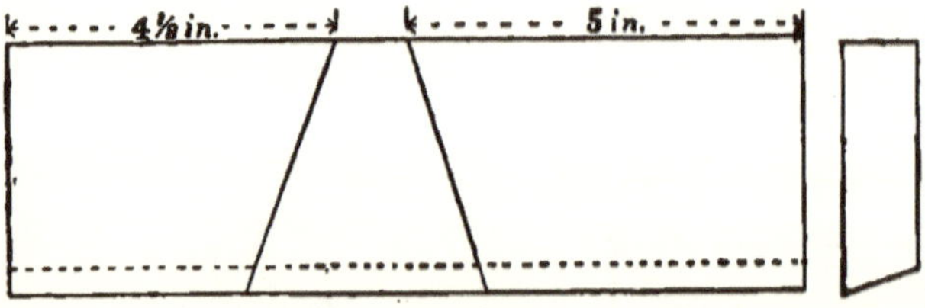

Fig. 183.

On the waste board, Fig. 181. make a second standard angle by making A E = 1 in. and A F = $3\frac{3}{16}$ in., and drawing E F. Set the bevel to this second standard angle, use it to draw the two bevelled lines shown in Fig. 183, continue these lines *square* across the bevelled edge of the work, use the bevel on the back side of the work, and finish by drawing such lines as are required, having a direction of their own on the squared edge. Saw near to the lines, plane exactly to them, and Fig. 183 will appear as Fig. 184.

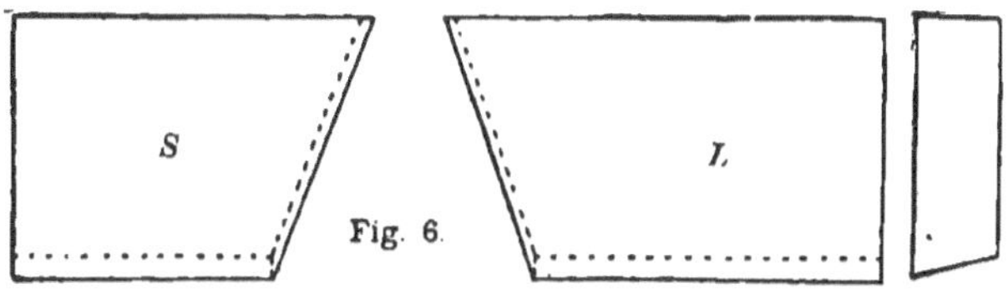

Fig. 184.

Brad-awl three holes in the longer piece L, giving them a direction parallel to the bevelled end and edge, and, using 2 in. No. 13 steel-wire finish nails, nail it to the shorter piece S. Cut away the small portion of L that now stands above the plane of the upper edge of S, and the work will appear as in Fig. 180.

Fold a small piece of No. ½ sand-paper over a small block, and sand the work, being careful not to disturb the corners. Apply a coat of clean, thin shellac, using a camel's-hair brush about 1¼ in. wide. Let it dry an hour or more, sand off all roughness, and apply a second coat of shellac.

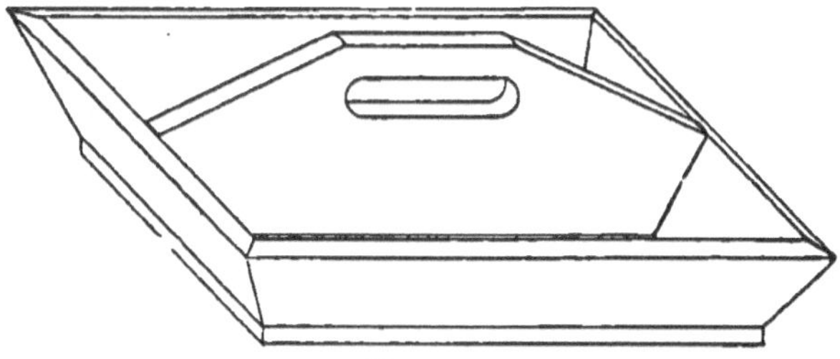

Fig. 185.

Problem II. The Bevelled Box. — Fig. 185 is a perspective view of the bevelled box which is made from ⅜ in. white wood. Fig. 186 is three orthographic views.

Draw an elevation of the angle full size, as in Fig. 187, and the slant height will be found to be $2\frac{1}{4}$ in.

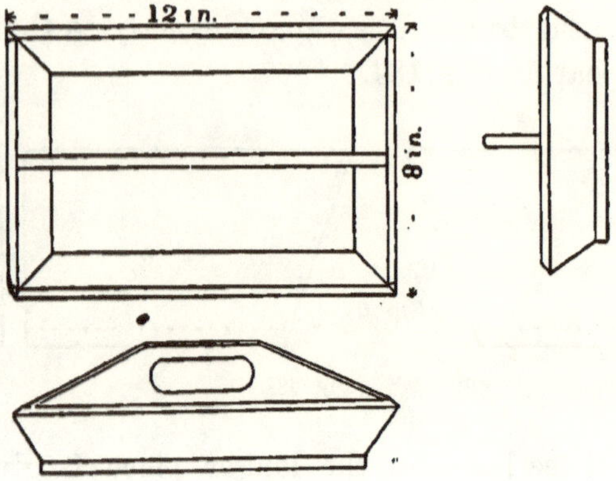

Fig. 186.

Make from $\frac{3}{8}$ in. white wood two side-pieces $12\frac{1}{2}$ in. rough length $\times$ $2\frac{1}{4}$ in. finish width, and two end-pieces 8 in. rough length $\times$ $2\frac{1}{4}$ in. finish width.

Take a waste board and lay out on it two standard angles, as in Fig. 188. Make $ab = 1$ in., and $ac = 2$ in. Set the

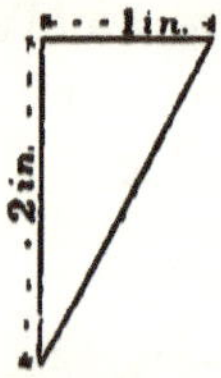

Fig. 187.

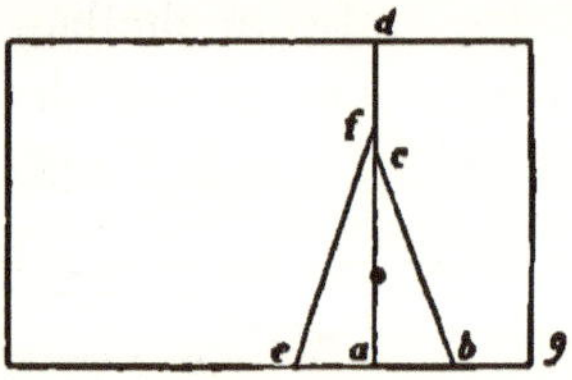

Fig. 188.

bevel to the line bc, and bevel the under edge of both side-pieces and both end-pieces. Make $ae = 1$ in., and $af = 2\frac{1}{4}$ in., set the bevel to the line ef, and lay out both ends of the four pieces in a manner similar to Problem I., making the two side-pieces each 12 in. long on the upper or square edge, and the two end-pieces $7\frac{1}{4}$ in. long on the upper or square edge. Saw near to the lines, and plane exactly to them.

Brad-awl three holes in each end of the side-pieces, in a manner similar to Problem I., and nail the four finished pieces together with $1\frac{1}{2}$ in. No. 16 steel-wire brads. Trim off the slight projections on each of the four upper corners, as was done in Problem I. Use a 22-in. iron jointer to make the lower edge of the frame more true. Make a board as long and as wide as the lower edge of the frame; on the upper side of this board scribe a line $\frac{3}{16}$ in., or one-half of the thickness of the stock, from each end and from each edge, as in Fig. 189.

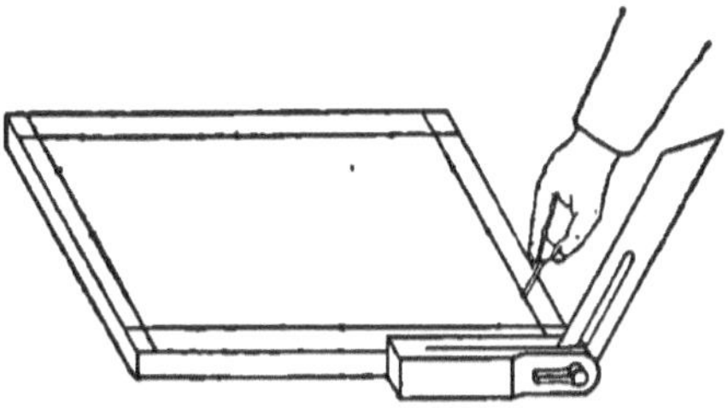

Fig. 189.

Fig. 192.

Bore three holes, the first one being an inch from the end, on each of these lines, using the bevel set to the angle *gbc*, Fig. 188, and located as in Fig. 189 to give direction to the awl. While doing this, keep the work on a waste board.

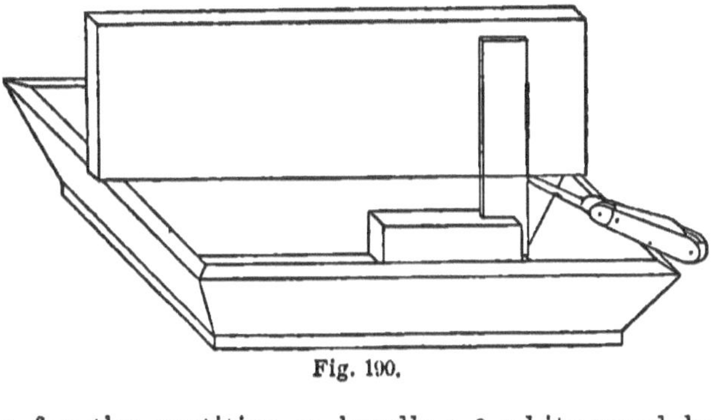

Fig. 190.

Make for the partition or handle a $\frac{3}{8}$ white wood board 12 in. rough length × $3\frac{3}{4}$ in. finish width. Place it on the box, as in Fig. 190, and placing the try-square as in that figure, make a knife-point on the under edge of the work. Repeat at the other end. The distance between these points is the length of the bottom of the box inside. From these points square across the under edge of the partition. With the bevel set by one end of the box, inside, finish laying out one end of the partition, then set the bevel by the opposite end of the box, and lay out the other end of the partition. Saw near to the lines, and plane exactly to them. The partition will appear as in the outline of Fig. 191.

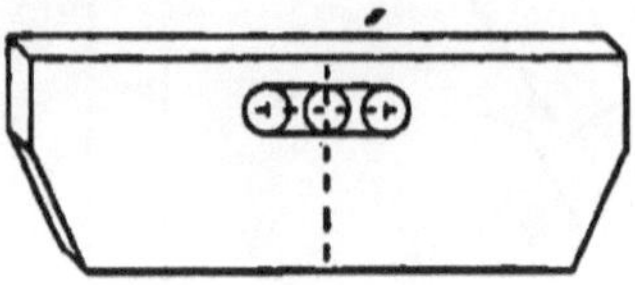

Fig. 191.

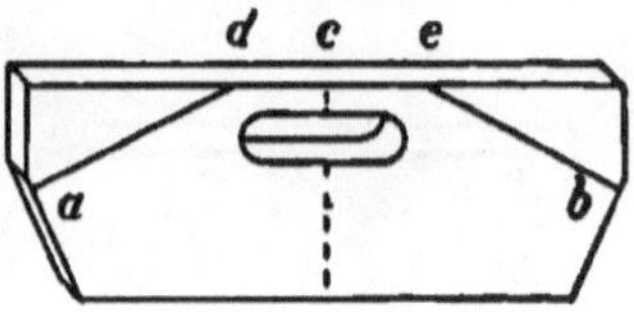

Fig. 193.

Find the middle point of the lower edge, and square up from it a fine pencil-line on one side of the board. Set the gauge 1 in., and gauge from the upper edge of the board on the same side a line about 1⅛ in. each way from the squared line. From the intersection of these lines, measure 1⅛ in. each way, and place two points on the gauge-line, as in Fig. 191. With these three points as centres, bore with the ¾ in. auger-bit three holes as shown by the circles on Fig. 191, till the spur of the bit is felt on the back side of the work, then turn the work over and bore from these points to meet the first boring. Set the gauge to agree with the upper and with the lower edges of the bored holes successively, and gauge lines on both sides. Cut to these lines with the small blade of the knife and round the edge of the cutting, as in the end view, Fig. 192, page 89.

Place the partition in position in the box, and make pencil-points at *a* and *b*, Fig. 193, where the upper edge of each end-piece of the box meets the partition. From *c* measure 1¾ in. each way on the upper edge of the partition, and place points at *d* and *e*. Draw the lines *ad* and *be*, saw near to them, and plane exactly to them. Round the edge *adeb*, as in the end-view of it, Fig. 192.

Nail the partition in place, using two 1-in. No. 18 steel-wire brads in each end, and three in the bottom.

Sand-paper the box, being careful of the corners. Stain it a neat cherry color, using burnt sienna thinned with turpentine, applied with a bristle brush, and rubbed off with cloth. After drying a few hours, shellac it as the joint was done.

Shellac may be used without staining, or the box may receive two coats of furniture varnish. If varnish is used, rub the first coat, when it has dried hard, with pumice and oil instead of sand-paper.

LESSON XVI.

GRINDING-TOOLS.

THE power of sharpening tools is superior to the power of using them; and though a few pupils may acquire it early in their practice of using tools, the majority of grammar pupils will need assistance from the teacher for some time, yet class instruction should be given, and individual practice had. To accomplish this, provide half a dozen cheap 1-in. shank chisels. Have, if possible, at least three grindstones, though one can be made to answer. One reason for mentioning three is that much grinding may be done, and another is that one stone may be kept for each of three varieties of work; viz., a coarse stone for plane blades and wide chisels, where much stock needs to be removed; a finer one for narrow chisels and knife-blades, and a third stone, also fine, for outside ground gouges. The inside ground gouges need an emery-wheel to grind them. Their use, however, in these lessons can be dispensed with.

All three stones may be used for chisels and planes indiscriminately when necessary, if kept trued, but the third stone is mentioned for gouge-grinding, as gouges make such grooves in a stone as to make it exceedingly difficult, if not impossible, for an amateur to use it for planes. For the coarse stone, the quarry at Norwalk, O., is excellent. For the finer ones, nothing excels Nova Scotia stone.

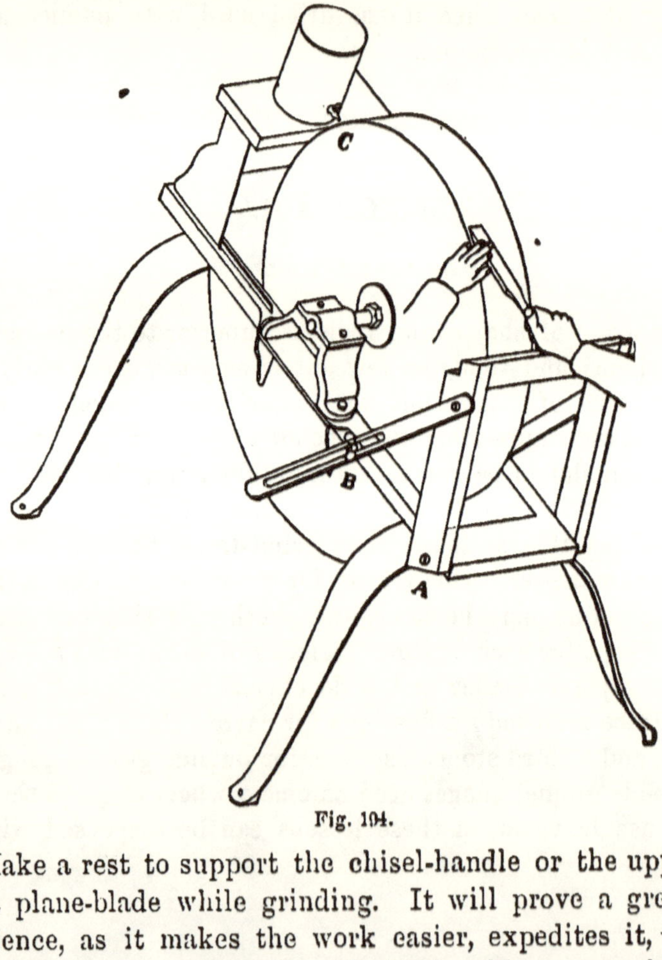

Fig. 194.

Make a rest to support the chisel-handle or the upper end of a plane-blade while grinding. It will prove a great convenience, as it makes the work easier, expedites it, and insures accuracy. An excellent device for this purpose is shown in Fig. 194, where a chisel is held in position for grinding.

The device is adjustable to hold any length of tool, from the shortest plane-blade to the longest chisel. Fig. 195 is a side view illustrating it more clearly. The rest pivots at A, while a slot and thumb-screw at B on each side give it adjustment and secure it. From a faucet in the copper pail at C, a stream of water of any needed size can be allowed to run. Aqueduct water, if available, will be more convenient. The smaller this stream the better; and, if it can be made to drop instead of run, it will be best. Have a box under the stone to catch waste water, and, if possible, a pipe to conduct from the box to a sewer.

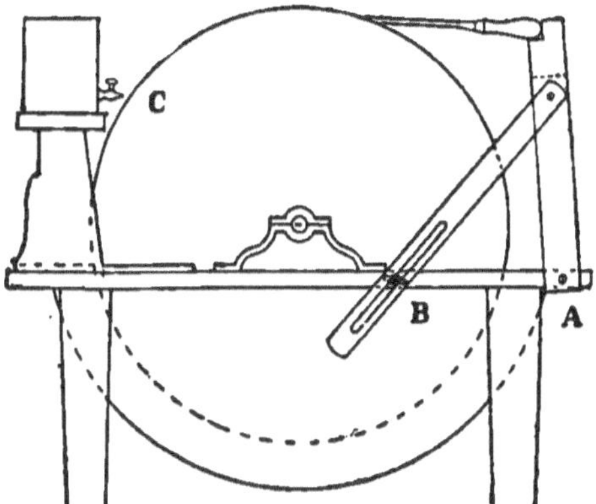

Fig. 195.

Do not hold a tool on a stone in one position continuously, as that tends to wear away the stone at that place, and consequently makes a groove in it. It also tends to make the edge of the tool irregular by its conforming to the irregularities of the stone. Keep the tool moving slowly to the right and left, as shown by dotted lines in the plan view, or diagram, Fig. 196.

A chisel may be swung to right and left, pivoting on the end of the handle at A, where it is supported on the rest; but

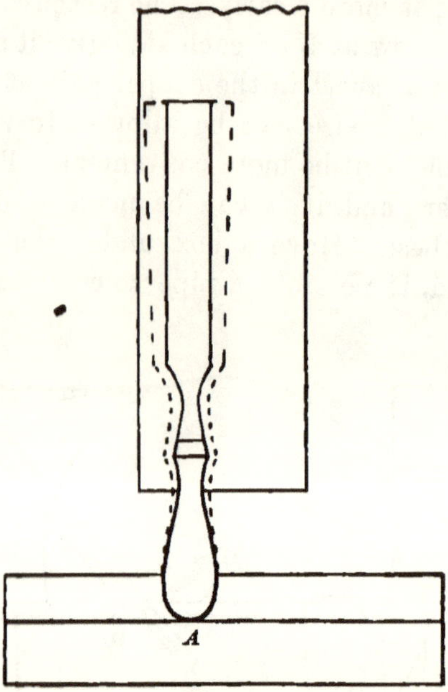

Fig. 196.

a plane-blade needs to be moved bodily, as shown by dotted lines, Fig. 197.

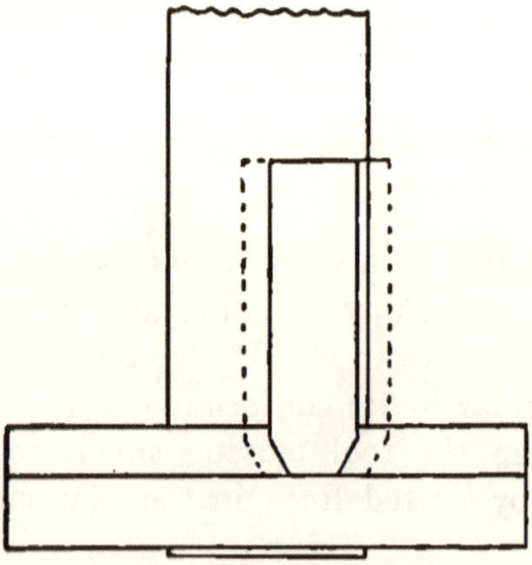

Fig. 197.

There is a natural tendency to use the middle of the face of a stone, as in the plan view, or diagram, Fig. 198.

The result of this is that most any stone in use will be found to have a hollowed face, as in the elevation, Fig. 199.

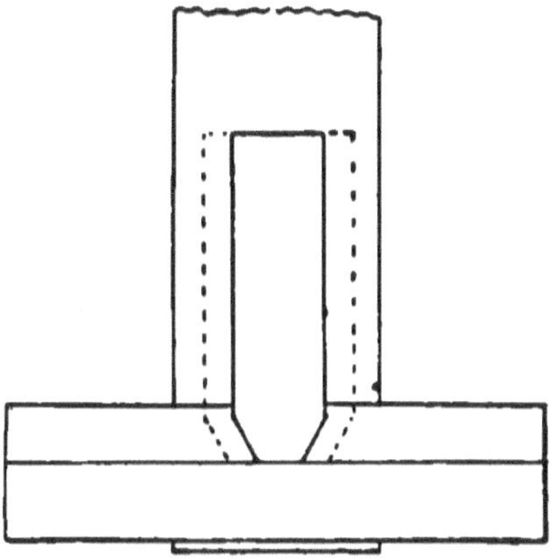

Fig. 198.

Fig. 199.

To obviate this as much as possible, always use the portion near one edge, as in Fig. 196 or 197, when you can.

In the process of grinding, particles of steel worn off from the tool fill the pores of the stone, and its surface becomes glossed so that it will not cut the tool readily. This will happen to any grindstone after an hour's constant use, and must be scraped off, as in Fig. 200, using for the purpose a bar of soft iron, preferably 1 in. × $\frac{3}{16}$ in. It will seem strange to the uninitiated that a bar of soft iron should be used for this purpose instead of steel, but such is the fact.

Not more than two or three minutes are needed for this duty, and it is surprising to note the difference in the cutting quality of the stone before and after the scraping.

When the face of a stone becomes so much out of true that a plane-blade cannot be ground on it, it must be trued either by means of a piece of flat-iron or gas-pipe handled by a skilful operator in a manner similar to Fig. 200, or preferably by means of some one of the truing devices which can be purchased and kept for the purpose.

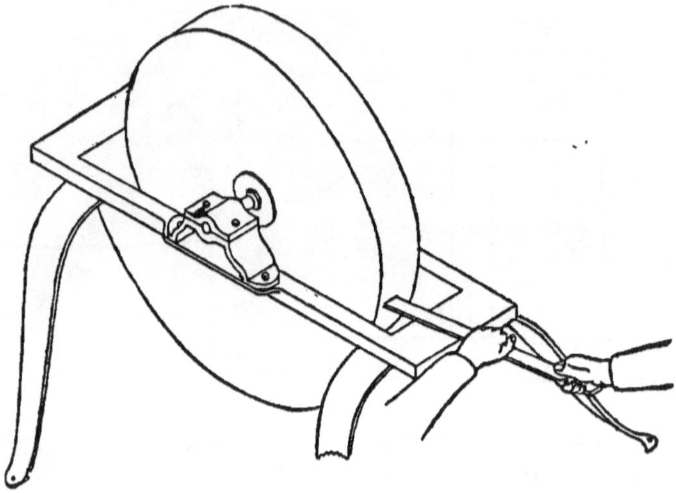

Fig. 200.

The form of the edge of different planes has been shown at Figs. 84 and 85.

The edge of a chisel should be ground straight as from *a* to *b* in Fig. 201.

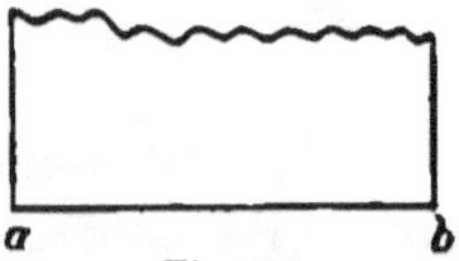

a *b*

Fig. 201.

After properly grinding a tool, put a smoother edge on it by means of an oil-stone. For common wood-working tools the article known as "Washita Stone" is excellent. "Arkansas Stone" is more expensive, having finer grain. It is specially adapted for small and fine-cutting tools. Fig. 202 is a side view of a chisel resting on a stone as it should in the act of stoning it. Keep the bevel of the tool in contact with the face of the stone, and then so strain the muscles that the front edge *a* shall be stoned without stoning the rear portion *b*.

Some stoning is necessary with the tool held flat side down,

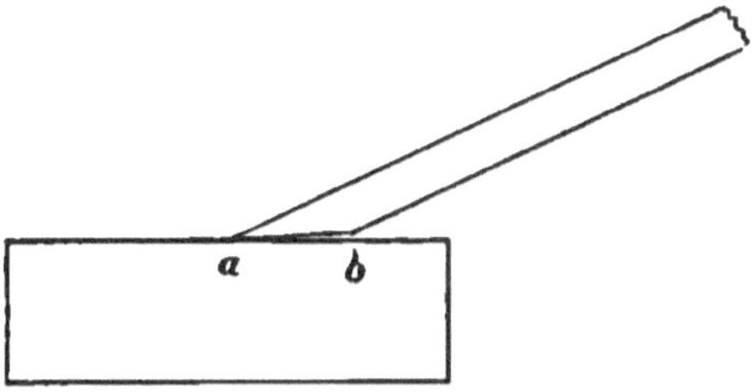

Fig. 202.

as in Fig. 203. Read also directions in connection with Fig. 48 concerning feather edges which sometimes occur.

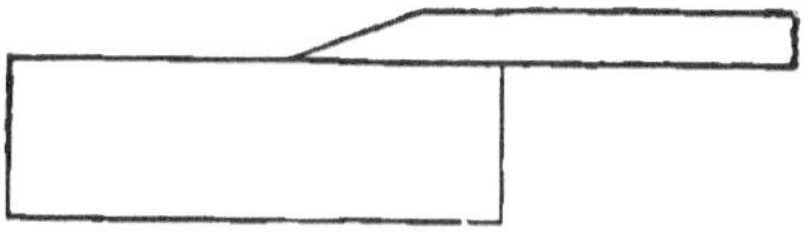

Fig. 203.

Grinding and stoning lessons may be given to sections of the class at any convenient time or times during the course of lessons.

After one of the cheap chisels mentioned has been put in good cutting order by a pupil, by grinding and oilstoning, it may be purposely dulled by striking the edge a few times with the peen hammer, and another pupil can then take a lesson in grinding it. After such nicking, whether purposely or accidentally done, place the chisel in a vertical position on the stone, as in Fig. 204, and grind the nicks out, then grind

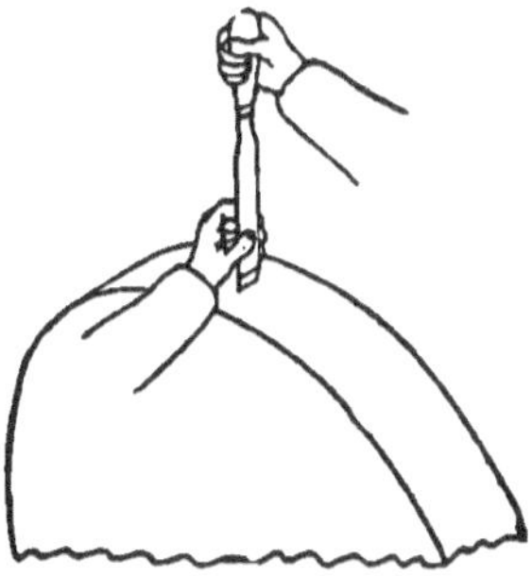

Fig. 204.

as in Fig. 194 to produce a new edge. Pupils who succeed with this experimental grinding can be trusted to put the regular tools in order when necessary.

There is the same natural tendency to use the middle portion of the face of an oilstone as of the grindstone, and the same constant endeavor is therefore needed to use portions near the ends and edges. When the surface of an oilstone becomes so untrue that planes cannot be stoned on it, tack a piece of No. 1½ sand-paper on a trued board, lay the oilstone on it face downward, and slide it in circular movements till it is sanded true. Time will be needed for this duty, and if the oilstone is much worn, several sheets of paper will be used.

A contrivance better than the sand-paper is a planed iron plate 12 in. square by ¾ in. thick. Put half a thimbleful of No. 90 emery on this plate, place the oilstone on it, and slide it with circular movements till the emery ceases to cut, which can be known by the sound, and then clean off the dust produced, and put on more emery. Each application of emery and grinding with it will occupy a moment or two, and the complete truing of the stone will occupy from fifteen minutes to an hour according to the amount of grinding needed.

To grind a knife requires more skill than to grind a chisel or plane, because its narrow blade furnishes so little convenience to rest it accurately.

In grinding it, let but a small portion of the length of the blade be in contact with the stone at a time, as in the front

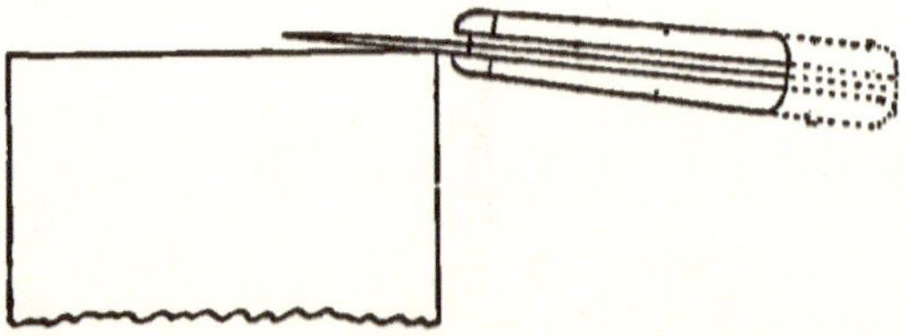

Fig. 205.

view, Fig. 205, but keep the knife constantly moving back and forth in the direction of its length, as indicated by the dotted lines.

The position Fig. 205 applies to grinding the straight portion of the blade, that is from *a* to *b*, Fig. 206.

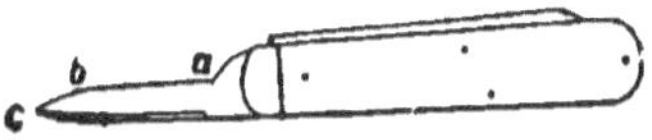

Fig. 206.

To grind the portion of the blade from *b* to *c*, hold it on the stone as in Fig. 207, giving it a continuous longitudinal and rocking motion, necessitated by its shape.

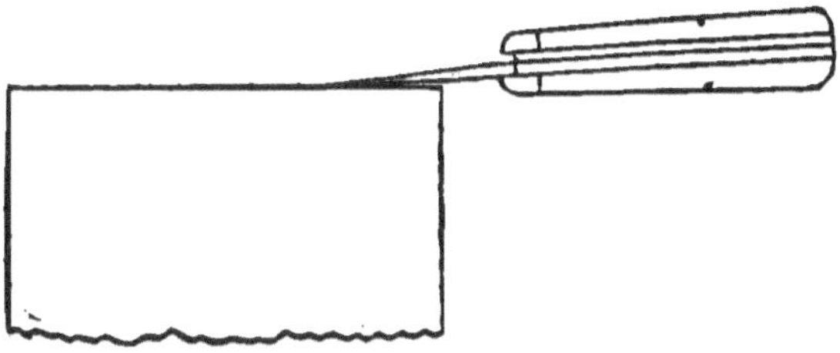

Fig. 207.

For directions concerning oilstoning the knife, see in connection with Figs. 46 to 48.

It will be noticed that the foregoing lessons give practice in using every tool or class of tools in the set enumerated, under the head of Equipment, pages 5 and 6, and, if thoroughly mastered, they will insure a complete elementary knowledge of hand woodwork, enabling an interested student to manufacture any simple article by applying the principles learned.

www.ingramcontent.com/pod-product-compliance
Lightning Source LLC
Chambersburg PA
CBHW032113010726
47493CB00008B/2561